ISBN 978-0-259-50671-3
PIBN 10820247

1 MONTH OF
FREE
READING

at

www.ForgottenBooks.com

By purchasing this book you are eligible for one month membership to ForgottenBooks.com, giving you unlimited access to our entire collection of over 1,000,000 titles via our web site and mobile apps.

To claim your free month visit:

www.forgottenbooks.com/free820247

THE

GIANTS OF PATAGONIA:

Captain Bourne's Account

OF HIS

CAPTIVITY AMONGST THE EXTRAORDINARY SAVAGES OF PATAGONIA.

WITH SIX FINE ENGRAVINGS.

TO WHICH IS ADDED, THE PAINFULLY INTERESTING NARRATIVE OF THE FATE OF THE PATAGONIAN SOCIETY'S MISSION IN TERRA DEL FUEGO.

LISTENING TO THE TICKING OF THE WATCH

LONDON: INGRAM, COOKE, AND CO.;
AND ALL BOOKSELLERS.
1853.

GIANTS OF PATAGONIA.

AMONG the early subjects of the "gold fever" that became epidemic in the autumn and winter of 1848-9, a company of twenty-five men left the port of New Bedford in the schooner John Allyne, A. Brownell, master, and B. F. Bourne, mate, for California. The vessel had been selected for her good sailing qualities, light draught of water, and general fitness for river navigation. In the haste and excitement of the time, California-bound craft carried out some rather motley companies ; but we considered ourselves fortunate in the character of the men associated in this enterprise, and were organized on such principles of equality as seemed to promise entire harmony and good fellowship. Of course we had high and golden hopes, and our great object was to reach the new Ophir in the easiest and most expeditious manner. On account of the delays and dangers incident to the doubling of Cape Horn, it was determined to attempt the passage of the Straits of Magellan.

We left port on the 13th of February, and for many days our time passed pleasantly, but rather monotonously, with nothing greatly to exhilarate or to depress our spirits. It was discovered, at length, that our vessel needed some running rigging. The more impatient were for going on, and making such headway as we could without it ; but a majority of the company decided to run for the nearest convenient port, and replenish. We accordingly ran for Pernambuco, and anchored in the outer harbour on the 25th of March. The beauty and security of this harbour are remarkable. It is defended from the sea by a nearly perpendicular reef, extending three-fourths of the way across its entrance, with an opening of ample width for the passage of vessels to a safe anchorage. Being but eight degrees south of the equator, the town lies continually under the burning rays of a tropical sun. Its appearance is like that of most Spanish and Portuguese cities, abounding in high and massive buildings, with more of the castle than of the counting-house or dwelling in their outward expression, built upon narrow, irregular streets, that are constantly alive with men and beasts of divers colours and forms. Men from the country, driving their mustangs, mules and asses, laden with produce ; wealthy and noble citizens borne by servants in palanquins ; women bearing water in buckets, tubs, and urns, which they balance on their heads without the aid of their hands, and walk off under as erect as so many midshipmen ;—all the sights and sounds have a pleasant strangeness, that made our visits on shore highly agreeable. The churches, which are quite numerous, have nothing admirable or attractive outside, but the richness of their interior decoration testifies to the prevailing orthodoxy and fervour of devotion to the Church of Rome. The church is, indeed, the grand receptacle of the wealth of the country. Every *bueno católico* of them, rich or poor, will sooner stint himself and his family in their daily comforts, or even necessaries of life, than omit his due contribution to mother church.

Our stay at Pernambuco was short, which must excuse a more particular description of its notabilities. Having obtained the articles we needed, we stood out to sea. Nothing occurred on our passage to the straits orthy of particular record. We spoke one or two sels, and spent some time " gaming" with them—the nautical phrase for visiting.　On the 30th of April we made Cape Virgin, and stood in for the Straits of Magellan.　In company with us, and bound for the same golden country, by the same course as ourselves, were bark Hebe, of Baltimore, and schooner J. B. Gager, of New York.　We were becalmed off the mouth of the straits for several hours, and Captain Brownell visited the Hebe.　He returned just before night.　A fair wind setting in from the eastward, we all stood in, the J. B. Gager, as being best acquainted with the navigation, taking the lead.　The three vessels anchored about midnight, within twelve miles of the first narrows.

The next morning, it being calm, some of our men went on shore in the small boat, for a gunning excursion.　They returned early in the forenoon, with a large number of seafowl.　Not long after, Captain Brownell announced his intention to go ashore, and commenced making preparations.　He soon changed his mind, however, and asked me to go in his stead, to procure some fresh provisions, if they were to be had.　Knowing, from the reports of whalers and others, something of the savage character of the natives, I felt reluctant to venture; but afterwards, to oblige the captain, I complied.

Taking our guns, a bag of bread, and some tobacco, four of us started for the shore.　As we approached the beach, a crowd of black-looking giants came to the water's edge to gaze at us.　We did not particularly fancy their looks, and lay on our oars for a considerable length of time.　A recollection of the many ugly stories current about the Patagonians, their barbarous and cruel character, did not greatly fortify our confidence, or make us especially anxious for a personal acquaintance with them.

We accordingly lay off in our boat, and hailing them in Spanish, asked them if they had eggs, fowls, and beef. They replied, in broken Spanish, that they had plenty at their houses.　I told them to produce their stores, and they should have plenty of bread in exchange.　We parleyed with them for some time, till our boat at length

safety first of all. Poor fellow ! I cannot blame him
for loving his own life, though, at the moment, it did
seem rather hard that, after getting into the scrape by
their own headstrong folly, against my entreaties and
peremptory commands, they should extricate themselves
from it at my expense, and leave me to bear the hardest
of it ! Very likely I might have done the same, if our
cases had been reversed. And, even if one of them had
offered to remain, it is very doubtful whether the sub-
stitution would have been permitted. The Indians too
evidently regarded me as the chief prize, and were bent
on retaining me as such. They insisted that I must
stay while the other three should go for ransom, and I
had nothing to do but to submit.

Three Indians each took a man with him on a horse,
and started for the boat. I watched them as they went,
with feelings that I will not attempt to describe. It
seemed but too probable we should never meet again.
A sense of desolation came over me, at the thought of
being left alone in the power of these savages, of whose
treachery and cunning I had already had such ample
experience, and of whose cruelty I had heard so much.
I felt that I was beyond the aid, if not cut off from the
sympathy, of my associates. The falseness of the
Indians to all their engagements, as I afterwards learned,
was signally displayed towards my more fortunate comrades. They evidently had no intention of releasing
any of us. Before reaching the boat, they halted, and
refused to go any further, or allow our men to leave
them. The prisoners, however, struggled desperately,
and at length got clear of their captors. One rushed up
to his neck in water, the others sprang into the boat,
pushed off, and rescued him as he was struggling with
the waves. They reached the schooner, told their tale,
and represented my desperate situation. All hands
commenced breaking up cargo, to get at the rum and
tobacco for my ransom. Two boats were forthwith
manned, provided with the required articles, and with

plenty of arms and ammunition, and started for the shore. They got to the land a little before dark, and pulled into a cove, or slight indentation of the beach.

On catching sight of them, I desired the Indians to conduct me to the shore, and receive the ransom. But this they declined. They ordered me to the summit of an eminence near by, there to beckon the men to come ashore. An old skin was given me to wave as a signal. Perceiving that I was to be used as a decoy to lure the others into their treacherous snare, and secure them all as prisoners, I protested against this new breach of faith, and assured them that our men would not leave their boat, but that, if they wanted any rum and tobacco, they must take me to the shore. To this, after a long palaver, and with visible reluctance, they assented. The old chief ordered me to mount his horse,—this time reversing our relative positions; he made me sit on the rude apology for a saddle and guide the horse, while he took his seat behind, clasping both arms tightly around my body, and spurring his old nag forward. Thus mounted, and wondering what would be the next trick of the savages, I was conveyed to the shore, near the spot where the boats lay off on their oars. Driving as near them as possible, I hailed the men,—told them by no means to fire on the Indians, but to give them all they had promised. They asked what they should do with the articles. I turned to the chief, told him what the boats had brought, and once more asked if it was a satisfactory ransom. He said, Yes; if those articles were laid down, I should be released. But he was plainly resolved to have his pay in advance; he distrusted us too much to let me go first; and I need not say that my confidence in him was far from implicit. But "Nothing venture, nothing have,"—I directed the men to put the things ashore, which they did. The Indians greedily picked them up, and I claimed my release. The old rascal said, "he had not got plenty of rum yet, he must have a barrel." I insisted and struggled, but to no purpose. He kept a tight hold of my body, and when I begged that at least he would not squeeze me quite so painfully, he only redoubled his clasp. He obviously suspected, and I more than suspected, that it would not require a very great relaxation of his embrace to prompt a pretty decided movement on my part, for the effectual resisting of which the vicinity of the water was not altogether favourable. He now began spurring his old horse from the scene of action; I drew upon the bridle with my whole available force and weight; but the disparity between human strength and horse power, stimulated to its utmost by the spur, was too great. I begged the men in the boats to come again the next morning, and on no account to leave me, which they solemnly promised.

I was now hurried back into the country five or six miles, and at last reached an Indian village, and was set down by the old chief at his wigwam. He gave me in charge to one of his squaws, who ordered me into the hut and bade me sit down on the ground. While sitting there, and casting an inquisitive glance around the rude habitation, my attention was suddenly attracted to what appeared to be several pairs of eyes in a dark corner, shining with a strange brilliancy. I speculated silently on the sight, much doubting whether they belonged to human beings or to wild beasts; but, on carefully reconnoitring, I discovered that they belonged to three huge women. Further investigations disclosed a number of dark-skinned boys and girls, of divers ages and sizes, playing and capering about the premises, in a state of perfect nudity. It took a considerable time to make out these, or any other objects, distinctly, owing to the darkness of the hut. Presently, the chief, the patriarch of the tribe, entered his habitation, and began a conversation, in his peculiar dialect, with his wives. He spoke in a low, guttural tone, in words, the purport of which I could not gather. I was in no mood for conversation, but would have been much gratified by learning his version of the day's " stroke of business."

And now a few dry sticks and a bunch of dry grass
were brought, mine host drew from a convenient repository a brass tinder-box, with a stone and a piece of
steel, and soon produced a blaze that brilliantly illumi-
nated the scene. By its light I was enabled to survey
the first specimen of Patagonian architecture that had
blessed my vision. It was constructed in a *pointed*
style, though not very aspiring, consisting of a row of
stakes about eight feet high, each terminating at top in
a crotch, or fork, with a pole laid across them; two
parallel rows of stakes on either side, about two feet
high, with similar terminations, and a similar horizontal
fixture; and a covering composed of skins of the
guanaco, sewed together with the sinews of the ostrich,
the only thread used by the people. This covering is
drawn over the frame-work, and fastened by stakes
driven through it into the ground. For purposes of
ventilation some interstices are left, but these again are
half closed by skins attached to the outside; so that the
air from without, and the smoke from within (in default
of a chimney), must insinuate themselves through these
apertures in great moderation. In truth, my first survey was rather hurried; the first cheerful gleam had
scarcely set my eyes on the look-out, when I was fain
to shut them against an intolerable smoke. In no long
time I felt as bacon, if conscious, might be supposed to
feel in the process of curing. No lapse of time was
sufficient to reconcile my eyes, nostrils, and lungs, to
the nuisance; often have I been more than half strangled
by it, and compelled to lie with my face to the ground,
as the only endurable position. Talk that is "worse
than a smoky house" must be something out of date, or
Shakspeare's imagination never comprehended anything
so detestable as a Patagonian hut. The chief and his
numerous household, however, seemed to enjoy immense
satisfaction; and jabbered and grunted, and played their
antics, and exchanged grimaces, as complacently as if
they breathed a highly exhilarating atmosphere.

My meditations and observations were shortly int

rupted by preparations for a meal. The chief's better-half—or rather fifth part, for he had four wives—super-intended the culinary operations, which were as rude and simple as the hut where they were carried on. And now my fancy began to conjure up visions of the beef, fowls, and eggs, the promise of which had lured my men from the boat—had proved stronger than the sug-gestions of prudence, and had made me a prisoner. But these dainties, if they existed anywhere within the chief's jurisdiction, were just at present reserved. The old hag threw down from the top of one of the stakes that supported the tent the quarter of some animal—whether dog, guanaco, or whatever, was past imagining. She slashed right and left, with might and main, an old copper knife, till it was divided into several pieces. Then, taking a number of crotched sticks, about two feet long, and sharpened at all their points, she inserted the forked ends into pieces of the meat, and drove the opposite points into the ground near the fire, which, though sufficient to smoke and comfortably *warm* the mess, was too feeble to roast it. At all events, time was too precious, or their unsophisticated appetites were too craving, to wait for such an operation; and the raw morsels were quickly snatched from the smoke, torn into bits by her dirty hands, and thrown upon the ground before us. The Indians seized them with avidity, and tossed a bit to me; but what could I do with it? I should have had no appetite for the dinner of an alderman at such a time and place; but as for tasting meat that came in such a questionable shape, there was no bringing my teeth or resolution to it. While eyeing it with ill-suppressed disgust, I observed the savages, like a horde of half-starved dogs, devouring their portions with the greatest relish; seizing the frag-ments with their fine white teeth, at the same time clenching them with their hands, and giving every sign of enjoyment *except* what one is accustomed to see in human beings. The old chief remarked the slight I was putting upon his hospitality, and broke in upon me with a fierce *Por que usted, no munge usted, usted carna? Esta carna mucho bueno hombre por munge, se hombre, munge!* "Why don't you eat your meat? This meat very good to eat—very good to eat. Eat, man! eat!" I may here observe that my knowledge of Spanish, like the chief's, was colloquial—picked up here and there in voyages to South American ports, which may account for my orthography being so plainly determined by the ear rather than by any rules of Castilian grammar. Seeing him so much excited, and not knowing what deeds might follow his words if I refused, I thought it expedient to *try* to "eat what was set before me, asking no questions;" thinking, moreover, that if there were any evil spirit in it that the fire had failed to expel, it could not possibly have resisted the smoke. So, being sorely divided between aversion to the "strange flesh" and fear of showing it, I forced a morsel into my mouth. Its taste was by no means as offensive as its appearance had been unpromising, and I managed to save appearances with less disgust than I had feared. This was my first meal with the savages, and a sample of many others; though better viands afterwards varied their monotony, now and then.

The eating being over, a large horn, that had once adorned the head of a Spanish bullock, was dipped into a leathern bucket and passed from one to another. Between the bucket and the horn, the fluid had gained a flavour not found by Adam in his first brewing, and, indeed, not far from nauseating. However, it seemed expedient to "conquer my prejudices" so far as to drink with the other guests, and the ceremonies of dinner were over; for which, "with all other mercies," I felt thankful, and turned to my corner near the expiring fire, to chew the cud of sweet and bitter fancies, in which the latter ingredient decidedly predominated. The strange and sudden desolateness of my condition, the doubtful chances of escape, the possible sufferings before me, the uncertainty that rested on the designs of my savage captors, all rushed upon my mind, and suggested to my heated imagination a host of terrors.

These painful thoughts were interrupted by an order to prepare for the night's repose. An old skin, about two and a half feet square, was thrown upon the cold ground in the back part of our rookery, and assigned for my couch: I took possession accordingly, and the whole family bestowed themselves in a row near me. The stifling atmosphere was soon vocal with their snoring. My brain was too busy for sleep. Feverish fancies kept me wakeful. I revolved a variety of plans for escape. Could I steal out of the hut unperceived? Could I find my way to the shore? I doubted the first, and more than doubted the second; and even if so far successful, there was no boat to take me from the accursed land. And how could I conceal myself from the Indians till a boat should arrive? They would miss me; and, long before any possible communication with my vessel, would be hunting me down with horses and dogs. Not a wood or thicket had met my eye on the dreary waste I traversed the day before. I tried to devise some other plan, but none offered itself. It was this or nothing—and this was next to nothing. Grown desperate, at last, I determined to make an effort.

After lying some time, listening to the heavy breathing of the sleepers, and satisfying myself that none of the company were awake, I raised myself as noiselessly as possible, and stole towards the front of the wigwam. Casting a furtive glance backward, I could see that the old chief was restless; either he had feigned sleep, or some evil spirit had waked him just at the wrong time. To go immediately back would too plainly betray my purpose; so I walked very calmly and deliberately into the open air, and stood as if star-gazing; the old fellow, as I plainly perceived, all the time watching me from the lodge. In a short time I walked quietly back to my dark retreat, and found him where I had left him, lying very cozily, as if nothing had happened to disturb his slumbers. Once more stretching myself on my uneasy couch, I lay two hours or more, still revolving the same unsolved problem in my mind. At length, all appearing to be sound asleep, I decided to venture a second attempt ; and, in the event of failure, to make the best of it for the present. Stealthily as possible I crawled from among them, slid out of doors, and crouched upon the grass. Could I be mistaken? No: those infernal eyes were fastened on me as before ! There was no eluding their vigilance. At this moment a howling as of a hundred wolves was heard approaching, and about that number of dogs came rushing, pell-mell, towards me. I scampered for the wigwam as fast as my feet could carry me, and in my flight stumbled over a stick nearly eight feet long. I seized the weapon thus kindly lent me, and, swinging it furiously about me, gave all intruders that came within my reach a sufficient touch of its quality. Thus defending myself from the brutes, I backed towards the lodge, glad to shelter myself among its detested inmates. The cunning old Parosilver, as before, had bestowed himself on the ground among his squaws and dirty children, and was apparently fast asleep.

This was more than I could compass. Vexation at my fruitless attempts to escape,—dread, inspired by the relentless vigilance and quiet assurance of the chief,— tormenting apprehensions as to the issue of any effort on the morrow to effect my ransom,—all kept my brain upon the rack, and effectually drove sleep from my eyes, till near daylight, when I fell into a disturbed slumber. In my dreams I was at once transported from the savage hut, on board my vessel. Methought she was driving before the wind, all sails set, at full speed, upon a dangerous reef. All on board seemed insensible of the danger ; I alone perceived it, but a nightmare spell was on me, and my lips refused to speak, my limbs to move. Rooted to my place on the deck, I stood in dumb agony,

while our vessel rushed upon her fate. There came a
sudden shock,—our bark had struck, and her total
destruction was inevitable. Some of the men were
dashed violently upon the deck, others precipitated into
the boiling surf, where they clung desperately to spars,
and fragments of the wreck. While the confusion was
wildest, and the dream of effort for escape was subsiding
into the calmness of despair, I suddenly awoke, and for
some time was unable to comprehend where I was, or
how I came there. If I were indeed shipwrecked, I was
also, like Jonah, vomited upon dry land. I drew my
hand across my eyes to assure myself that vision was
unobstructed, cast my eyes right and left;—the lodge,
the ashes of the last night's fire, the chief and his motley
family, the door through which the "lubber fiend" had
followed me with his restless eyes, and into which the
fierce dogs had driven me, recalled my distracted senses,
and restored consciousness of a reality which, at the
moment, I would almost have exchanged for the wildest
terrors of my dream.

With the light calmer thoughts succeeded, and I once
more addressed myself to the task of effecting my escape.
The first thing was to get the chief with me to the shore,
in readiness to meet a boat, and to renew negotiations
for my liberty. Observing that he was awake, I began
to promise him an abundant supply of the articles most
tempting to his fancy, on condition of my release. He
carelessly replied that he would go with me to the beach
by and by. I tried to urge his departure, being anxious
to go without the rabble at his heels the day before, but
for whose violence he would now hardly be master of
me; but there was no hurrying his movements. He
took down his little cutlass, drew it from its brazen
scabbard, and commenced sharpening it with a rusty
file, trying its edge with his fingers as the work went on,
and casting side glances at me the while. Whether this
ceremony was the preface to some act of violence he
meditated, or a scene for effect, to fill me with a whole-

some dread of his power I could not guess; but, determined to show no foolish fears, I thought it best to put a bold face upon the matter, and make an equally striking demonstration of courage and presence of mind, qualities which savages generally appreciate. I therefore approached him, tried the edge with my own fingers, praised the beauty of the instrument, and interested myself in the process of sharpening it. Following up my assault on his vanity, I extolled him as one of the best of men, and assured him that when we got to the shore I would amply reward him for his kindness to me; taking occasion, however, to throw in a hint on the vast importance of starting early. This I enforced by the suggestion that, when he got his good things, the fewer there were present, the fewer claimants there would be to divide the spoils.

After much coaxing, he started after his old horse; I mounted behind him, and we moved slowly off. When we arrived at the shore it was blowing a perfect gale. A boat could not live in the billows. All three vessels had dragged their anchors, and lay at some distance from their anchorage of yesterday. Bark Hebe appeared to be dragging towards the Orange Bank, a dangerous shoal. I afterwards learned that the Hebe, after getting into water as shoal as would barely float her, slipped her cables, put up a little sail, and finally succeeded in weathering the shoal and getting safely out to sea. The J. B. Gager was dragging in the same direction. My own vessel was holding on better than the others, and I hoped she would ride out the gale in safety.

I made my captors understand the reason why no boat had come, as promised; with which they appeared to be satisfied, and we returned as we came. By means of their broken Spanish, which they had picked up from sailors, and in visits to the Chilian or other Spanish American settlements, and by signs, amounting at times pretty nearly to a pantomime, I found myself able to understand inquiries or commands, and to make known my wishes.

Early on the following morning we again visited the shore, and I looked eagerly towards the anchorage, where all my hopes of deliverance centred. Not a vessel was in sight. Whether they had foundered, or were driven upon the shoal and wrecked, or had dragged out to sea in a disabled condition,—or whether my shipmates, the gale having subsided, had deliberately proceeded on their voyage, and left me a prey to cruel savages, and all the ills of this inhospitable shore.—I was unable to conjecture. I only knew that they were gone, and that I was left alone to the tender mercies of the Patagonians. No present means of escape appeared. The future, wisely hidden from my view, suggested none to my imagination. I told my captors the worst; that the high winds had probably sunk the ships, and all that were in them. At this intelligence, they seemed delighted, and laughed immoderately, as if such a calamity were a consolation for the loss of their expected ransom. Their cruel glee could add nothing to the weight of my desolation. My past life was sealed up as if by an entrance on a new state of being. I looked round on a bleak and cheerless region, and forward on a life as barren of human joy, made up of every species of suffering,—hunger, cold, fatigue, insult, torture,—liable to be cut short at any moment by the caprice of my tormentors, and so wretched that death itself, with all the enormities of cannibalism, lost its terrors by comparison. Life, for any good or great purposes to be achieved, was over. And then my thoughts turned to far different scenes,—to happy faces, and pleasant voices, and familiar sights;—to hearts that beat with no dread of this day's calamities, felt no consciousness kindred to my despair, but would in due time, be rudely awakened from their security. God help me, for I am helpless now.

CHAPTER II.

RETURNING to the encampment, it remained to devise some new way of escape. Some four or five days' ride to the westward would bring us to Port Famine, on the straits, a penal settlement of Chili, and the only settlement in the vicinity by which I could hope to reënter the civilized world. A journey thither was suggested to the Indians, as the most likely way of turning my captivity to profitable account; but they refused with a promptness and decisiveness which was rather unaccountable, till I afterwards learned that they had lately visited that part of the country on a horse-stealing expedition, in which their success had been too good to make them desirous of showing their faces there at present. Money, guns, pistols, cutlasses, brass, beads, and everything else that could be thought of to tempt their cupidity, were offered. I was not disposed to be niggard of promises; but in vain. To Port Famine they were determined *not* to go; but old Parosilver assured me, by way of compensation, that he would take me to "Holland," which was a "much better place." Whereabout on terra firma this South American Holland was situated,—if, indeed, there was any such place, and the chief was not indulging in a little extra lying,—was past all conjecture. I inquired the distance. He could not tell exactly. Was it inhabited by Americans or English? There were "twenty or thirty white men there, and plenty of rum and tobacco." They promised to start with me towards Holland the next day. In what direction? They pointed towards the Atlantic. Well, I cared little where it was, or who lived there, provided only they were not Patagonians, and I could once get free of these rascals. But on the following morning the migration was postponed, in consequence of unexpected tidings.

One of the tribe, who had been down to the shore, reported that my vessel had come back. This welcome, though rather improbable information, started me, with about a dozen of them, on the track of his story. On gaining a view of the straits, a vessel was plainly in sight, but it was a strange sail. Yet, if I could succeed in boarding her, my purposes would be answered. She came into the bight of the bay, and anchored about fifteen miles below us. I endeavoured to make my smutty companions comprehend that as the tide was then running out they would not make the shore till it turned, which would not be till night. They waited till near night, when hunger and thirst wore out their patience, and they ordered me off with them. Against this untimely mandate I warmly remonstrated, and after some dispute it was arranged that the chief should stay with me for the night. The rest returned to their encampment, and we made a good fire, which was kept up till nearly morning. Old Parosilver lay down under the lee of a clump of bushes, while I was busy in active exercise to keep warm, and replenishing the fire with dry bushes. At dusk I had observed the vessel hoisting sail, and beating up the bay. On this I began brandishing firebrands to attract notice, and walked to and fro on the beach for hours. The craft gradually approached, till her white canvas became distinguishable through the surrounding gloom. Fresh fuel was heaped on the fire, a bright blaze ascended ; I took my station directly in front of it, holding out my coat, and frequently turning round, that my form and features might be more distinctly revealed. And now a thrill of joy electrified me, as I saw a light set on deck, which appeared to be stationary. There could be no doubt that the vessel had come to anchor directly opposite to us. Though hungry and weary with long watching, I hurried about, and gathered sticks and leaves in abundance to kindle a still brighter beacon-fire, in whose light and warmth anxiety began to expand into hope. At dawn of day, as the horizon lighted up, I could distinguish the vessel lying about a mile off, quiet as a sea-fowl on the calm surface. Presently there was a movement on deck, the anchor was hove up, the fore and main sails were hoisted, and the object on which my hopes and ardent prayers had centred through the cold night receded from view through the straits, bound, doubtless, for California. I watched the fast-vanishing sail with tearful eyes; and the old chief, who had been on the look-out, started for his horse, that had been hampered and turned out to crop among the scanty vegetation.

Before I had time to recover from the first revulsion of disappointment and grief, *another* vessel, a topsail schooner, came in by Point Dungeness. "Cheer up," I said to myself; "the sun will be shining, the darkness have given place to the clear day, before this vessel can be up and opposite to us." Confident of being noticed, I began active preparations for the approaching visitor. No rod of sufficient length was to be found; but, after some search, a number of short, crooked sticks were collected. To lash them together, I tore up my drawers, which I could ill afford, and appropriated my shoe-strings. My flannel shirt was hoisted as a flag; and having replenished the fire, I paced the beach with colours flying, but, as the vessel approached, with increasing faintness of heart; for the wind gradually shifted, so that she could only take advantage of it by heading towards Terra del Fuego. At last she came opposite, but so near the further shore that the chances of success diminished every moment. Dark objects moved on the deck,—fancy painted them as men;—would they not discover me through their glasses, and be drawn by my signal of distress? No; onward she floated away,—the narrows were soon passed, and my vision of deliverance was dissipated.

With this final death-blow to all present hopes of relief, I turned away in despair. Exhausted by hunger, cold, and fatigue, and worn out by hours of anxiety, I

fell helpless upon the ground, and wept like a child.
For the first time I felt *utterly* forsaken, and repined at
my lot as one of unmitigated evil. Effort seemed useless; I had neither resolution nor strength to make
further exertion. There was nothing for me but listless
endurance. I even reproached myself that I had not
cast myself into the sea, and staked my life on the
chance of swimming to the schooner. There was no
possibility of doing this; but failure would have been
only death, and what was life worth to me here? This
tempest of self-reproach soon spent itself. My tempera-
ment is too buoyant to be long depressed, and calm and
stout thoughts took the place of despairing weakness.
It was unmanly, something whispered within me, thus
to give way before difficulties. It would be time enough
to do this when all possible effort had failed. The weak
and imbecile might take refuge in despair, but the
strength of youth should serve me better. I called to
mind examples of courage in greater emergencies, when
obstacles that seemed insurmountable had been con-
quered by fortitude and perseverance. "Heaven helps
those who help themselves." The more I reflected on
the matter, the stronger grew the impulses of faith and
courage, by whose force it seemed possible to win a
triumph against the greatest odds. Before rising from
the earth, my resolution was fully taken to throw discouragement to the winds; by the help of God to meet
whatever impended with the courage of a man; to bear
my calamities with patient endurance; and to give up
hope and energy only when nothing was left to be
attempted, or the power to do and suffer was exhausted.

I rose a new man,—my strength invigorated, my soul
fortified by a strong purpose. Though the cold night-
air had thoroughly chilled my frame, it now felt a warmth
kindled by the fires within, and an unaccustomed flush
suffused my countenance. The resolve fixed by this
memorable crisis of my captivity, though severely tested,
was never wholly overborne. Henceforth, the events

and scenes through which I passed were viewed with a calmness that had been before unattainable, and which is now scarcely credible, on recollection. So true is it that our strength is unknown to ourselves till it is thoroughly tested.

The hope of immediate release, however, was at an end; my savage captors, it seemed, must be looked upon as for an indefinite period my masters and companions; and I had nothing at present to do but to divert myself by a study of their manners and habits; to consult my safety by a close study of their character, and of the ways and means by which so to adapt my deportment to it as to win their confidence, to disarm hostility, and to seize opportunities.

PATAGONIA, as it offered itself to my observation, more than answered the descriptions of geographers,—bleak, barren, desolate, beyond description or conception,— only to be appreciated by being seen. Viewed from the Straits of Magellan, it rises in gentle undulations or terraces. Far as the eye can reach, in a westerly direction, it assumes a more broken and hilly appearance, and long ranges of mountains, extending from north to south, divide the eastern from the western shore. The soil is of a light, sandy character, and bears nothing worthy the name of a tree. Low bushes, or underwood, are tolerably abundant, and in the valleys a coarse, wiry grass grows luxuriantly. Streams of water are rare. The natives draw their supplies principally from springs or pools in the valleys, the water of which is generally brackish and disagreeable.

The variety of animal is nearly as limited as that of vegetable productions. The guanaco, a quadruped allied to. the lama, and with some resemblance to the came-leopard, is found in considerable numbers. It is larger than the red deer, fleet on the foot, usually found in large herds, frequently not only in the plains, but along the course of the Andes. Its flesh is a principal article of food; its skin is dried with the hair on, in such a manner that, when wet, it retains its pliability and soft- ness. This process of preserving skins seems to be peculiar to the Indian tribes, and is not unlike that by which buffalo robes, bearskins, buckskins, and other articles of luxury, and even necessity, among us, are prepared by the North American Indians. Guanaco- skins are cut into pieces of all sizes, and sewed into a thousand fanciful patterns, every workman originating a style to suit himself. The hoofs are sometimes turned to account by the natives as soles for shoes, when they indulge in such a luxury, which is not often.

The enemy of the guanaco is the cougar, or "American lion," smaller than its African namesake, and more re- sembling the tiger in his character and habits, having a smooth, sleek coat, of a browniish-yellow colour,—alto- gether a very beautiful but ferocious creature. His chase is a favourite, though rare and dangerous, sport of the natives. Patagonia likewise boasts of the skunk, whose flesh is used for food. There are also foxes, and innu- merable mice. Of birds, the only noticeable varieties are the condor, in the Andes, and the cassowary, a species of ostrich, smaller than that of Africa, on the plains; its plumage is not abundant, generally of a gray or dun colour. Its flesh is tender and sweet, and with the fat much prized by the Indians. Like the African ostrich, it is exceedingly swift, only to be captured on horseback, and often fleet enough to outrun the fastest racer.

The climate is severe. The Rio Negro forms the northern boundary, and nearly the whole country is south of the parallel of 40° south latitude. At the time of my capture, which was in the month of May, the weather corresponded to that of November in the New England States. Its chilliness, however, was greatly increased by the bleak winds of that exposed locality. Along the Straits of Magellan the weather is also exceedingly changeable. Sudden and severe squalls

often amounting almost to a hurricane, vex the navigation of the straits, and sweep over the coast with fearful
fury.

The habits of the Pantagonians, or at least of the
tribe among whom I was cast, are migratory, wandering
over the country in quest of game, or as their caprice
may prompt them. They subsist altogether on the
flesh of animals and birds. The guanaco furnishes most
of their food, and all their clothing. A mantle of skins,
sewed with the sinews of the ostrich, fitting closely about
the neck and extending below the knee, is their only
article of dress, except in the coldest weather, when a
kind of shoe, made of the hind hoof and a portion of
the skin above it, serves to protect their inferior extremities.

In person they are large; on first sight, they appear
absolutely gigantic. They are taller than any other
race I have seen, though it is impossible to give any
accurate description. The only standard of measure-
ment I had was my own height, which is about five
feet ten inches. I could stand very easily under the
arms of many of them, and all the men were at least a
head taller than myself. Their average height, I should
think, is nearly six and a half feet, and there were
specimens that could have been little less than seven
feet high. They have broad shoulders, full and well-
developed chests, frames muscular and finely propor-
tioned, the whole figure and air making an impression
like that which the first view of the sons of Anak is
recorded to have made on the children of Israel. They
exhibit enormous strength, whenever they are sufficiently
aroused to shake off their constitutional laziness and
exert it. They have large heads, high cheek-bones,
like the North American Indians, whom they also
resemble in their complexion, though it is a shade or
two darker. Their foreheads are broad, but low, the
hair covering them nearly to the eyes ; eyes full, generally black, or of a dark brown, and brilliant, though

expressive of but little intelligence. Thick, coarse, and stiff hair protects the head, its abundance making any artificial covering superfluous. It is worn long, generally divided at the neck, so as to hang in two folds over the shoulders and back, but is sometimes bound above the temples, by a fillet, over which it flows in ample luxuriance. Like more civilized people, the Patagonians take great pride in the proper disposition and effective display of their hair. Their teeth are really beautiful, sound and white,—about the only attractive and enviable feature of their persons. Feet and hands are large, but not disproportionate to their total bulk. They have deep, heavy voices, and speak in guttural tones,—the worst guttural I ever heard,—with a muttering, indistinct articulation, much as if their mouths were filled with hot pudding. Their countenances are generally stupid, but, on closer inspection, there is a gleam of low cunning that flashes through this dull mask, and is increasingly discernible on acquaintance with them; when excited, or engaged in any earnest business that calls their faculties into full exercise, their features light up with unexpected intelligence and animation. In fact, as one becomes familiar with them, he will not fail to detect an habitual expression of "secretiveness" and duplicity, which he will wonder he did not observe sooner. They are almost as imitative as monkeys, and are all great liars; falsehood is universal and inveterate with men, women, and children. The youngest seem to inherit the taint, and vie with the oldest in displaying it. The detection of a falsehood gives them no shame or uneasiness. To these traits should be added a thorough-paced treachery, and, what might seem rather inconsistent with their other qualities, a large share of vanity, and an immoderate love of praise. They are excessively filthy in their personal habits. Hydrophobia, so to speak, is a prevailing distemper; they never wash themselves. Hands and faces are covered with dirt, so thick, and of such ancient deposit, that their natural

colour only appears in spots, laid bare by the mechanical
loosening and displacement of some of the strata, which
curiously variegate the surface. It is hardly necessary
to remark that such a condition of the skin is highly
favourable to the increase and multiplication of "the
moving creature that hath life," wherewith their persons
are abundantly peopled.

The women are proportionally smaller than the men,
and rather inclined to embonpoint. The old chief had
four wives, though he had probably never heard of
Mahomet or his domestic laws. The rest of the tribe
had only one wife apiece. The women erect the wigwams, provide fuel, and cook,—if the operation should
be dignified with that name,—in short, all the drudgery
falls to their lot. They are treated as slaves, but made,
in most respects, as comfortable in their servitude as
the condition of their rude masters will admit. When,
however, their lords are excited by gambling, or enraged
for any or no cause, the fury of passion is visited upon
their defenceless heads, which they bear uncomplainingly,
with a meek submissiveness worthy of better treatment.
They are passionately fond of trinkets and clumsy ornaments, such as bits of brass and copper, beads, and the
like, which they wear suspended from their necks. A
few of them had their ears pierced, and wore brass or
copper ear-rings ; and many of them decked out their
children with similar rude finery, which is valued more
than anything else, except rum, tobacco, and bread.
The men paint or bedaub their faces and breasts with a
kind of red earth. Charcoal is also used as a cosmetic.
A broad line of red alternating with a stripe of black,
in various fantastic figures, is a favourite style of decoration. The women make themselves, if possible, still
more hideous, by the application of a pigment made of
clay, blood, and grease. Some of them would be very
comely, if only cleanly, and content to leave nature less
strenuously adorned.

The people are as deficient in the morals as in the

refinements and courtesies of domestic life; their licen-
tiousness is equal to their cruelty,—the filth of their
persons only too faithfully represents the degree in which
" their mind and conscience is defiled." I saw no person, of either sex, that appeared to have attained
advanced age, though it was difficult to judge of this.
The oldest Indian I remember to have seen did not
seem to be above sixty.

Their only wealth, aside from their huts, consists of
horses, the stock of which is frequently replenished by
stealing from the Spanish and Chilian settlements.
These animals are, for the most part, of small size and
inferior quality, half wild, coated with coarse, shaggy
hair—lean and wobegone enough, just "fit for the
crows." A few valuable specimens of a superior breed
are found among them, doubtless "conveyed" there.
The rude saddles in use among them are mostly of
Spanish origin, obtained at the settlements. They con-
sist each of two boards, an inch thick, six inches wide,
and two feet long, rounded at the corners so as to fit the
horse's back, and united by two strips of board passing
across the back-bone, the several pieces lashed together
with leather strings. A piece of guanaco-skin often
serves in default of a saddle. The steed is guided by
a single rein, tied round the lower jaw; some of them
sport a bit of iron or wood, secured by a string round
the jaw, attaching the rein to this. Spurs, like the rest
of their riding apparatus, are more efficient than elegant.
They are, indeed, rude and cruel things,—straight sticks,
six inches long, with a long, sharp iron inserted into the
end, secured by a string or strap around the hollow of
the foot, and tied at the top, a second strap nearer the
heel, and a third passing round the heel. They are all
agile and excellent horsemen.

For weapons, the chief, and a few of the principal
men, had cutlasses or swords. They had no fire-arms,
nor could I learn that they understood their use; bows
and arrows, spears and war-clubs, appeared to be equally

o

PATAGONIANS.

unknown. All the men carried knives ; and the *bolas*, a missile weapon used in the capture of all kinds of game. This consists of two round stones, or lead balls, if they can be procured, weighing each about a pound, connected by a strap or thong of leather, ten or twelve feet long. When engaged in the chase, his horse at his highest speed, the rider holds one ball in his hand, and whirls the other rapidly above his head; when it has acquired a sufficient momentum it is hurled with unerring aim at the object of pursuit, and either strikes the victim dead, or coils inextricably about him and roots him to the spot, a helpless mark for the hunter's knife.

The tribe numbered about one thousand ; the chief is the acknowledged head of the people. Whether his power was hereditary or elective, I could not learn; but incline to the belief that it was hereditary, as it appeared to be, in his theory at least, absolute. In all questions of importance his decision is final; yet his subjects take considerable liberty with his opinions, sometimes oppose his counsels, and even question his authority. On the appearance of such democratic symptoms, he sometimes finds it necessary to assert his sovereignty with spirit, and brandishes his cutlass smartly before their eyes.

The habits of the people are not only filthy, but indolent to the last degree; exertion of body or mind is their greatest dread. They never go on a hunting expedition till there is nothing more to eat, nor even then till they feel the spur of extreme hunger. It sometimes happens that at such a crisis a storm comes on, which shuts them in ; and it is no unfrequent occurrence for them, under such circumstances, to pass two or three days without tasting food. They learn nothing by experience; the same childish indolence and recklessness, followed by the same painful consequences, are continually recurring.

Though their great size at first sight was fitted to inspire terror, it required no very long observation to discover that they were deficient in natural courage. This,

in fact, might be inferred at once, from their habitual
deceit, treachery, and artifice, which are the defences of
the weak and timorous, rather than the weapons of
strong and daring natures. They always select night to
inflict injuries; never meet an enemy in open combat
whom they can stab from behind, or despatch in the
dark; and, when obliged to attack by day, always do so
in large numbers. This defect of courage is increased by
their superstition; they have great faith in charms, signs,
and omens, a weakness which I anticipated might exert
great influence on my destiny in important conjunctures:
Could I by any means so master their secret as to
possess myself of its mystic power, it might prove an
effective aid to my plans of self-defence, or of escape.
Should it, on the other hand, be turned by any acciden-
tal causes against me, its impulse might prove irresistible
by power or contrivance. There was no appearance
of idolatrous worship among them, nor could I observe
any allusion to a Supreme Being, or to any superior
powers having personal attributes; and, except a single
ceremony, of which more hereafter, the nature of which
was and is still inexplicable, there was nothing that
suggested to my mind the idea of religious worship.
Whether they are cannibals or not, has been a matter of
some dispute. So far as I know, they have been,
heretofore, only casually observed on the beach by
voyagers, or vaguely reported of by the people of adjoin-
ing countries and neighbouring settlements; neither of
which is a sufficiently reliable source of information.
My own personal advantages on this head were greater;
but I am obliged, after all, to leave the question about
where I found it, so far as *certain* conclusions are concerned. Yet some circumstances occurred, or were
related to me, that incline my mind strongly to the
belief that such horrible practices are not unjustly
ascribed to them. Of the soundness of my conclusions
those who follow the course of the narrative will have
the opportunity of judging for themselves; if such had
been my persuasion at the beginning, it may be readily

imagined what effect this last hazard would have had upon my feelings, in contemplating the possibilities of the future. Happily a convenient scepticism on this point preserved me from this dark apprehension.

I came among these people not, certainly, with the best preparation in my previous habits and associations to endure either the climate of the country or the hardships of captivity. I went on shore in my usual ship's dress; thick frock coat, trousers, and shoes, and glazed cap. My under-garments were woollen; though an important item, as before related, was made away with in fruitlessly signalling vessels in the straits. But to live without any change of dress, to sleep without any additional covering, protected from the cold ground only by a fragment of guanaco-hide, and the other discomforts and exposures of life among savages, made, altogether, a harsh contrast to the comforts of our good schooner. To these, however, I gradually became inured, till I was able to meet cold and wet and storm with as stoical indifference as my dark companions, who had known no other lot from infancy.

Of the character of the natives I had little previous knowledge; and that little was not adapted to stimulate curiosity, or prompt the least anxiety for more intimate acquaintance. It was derived mainly from whalers, in whom it seemed to have produced much the same degree of contentment,—a feeling that ignorance is bliss. Indeed, the greatest caution has always been employed by voyagers in regard to landing on these shores; many experienced seamen cannot be persuaded to land at all; trade with the natives is always carried on in boats off shore, frequently with loaded fire-arms constantly levelled, in readiness for action in case of emergency. But here I was, put forcibly to the study of their character in the school of dame Experience, and can testify to the truth of the saying that she charges roundly for tuition. Let the reader give me credit for the cheapness with which I put him in possession of what knowledge was purchased at so exorbitant a price.

CHAPTER III.

THE reader left me just rising from a half-stupor into which a double disappointment had thrown me, feverish with the excitement of new purposes and resolutions. The first aim was for some fresh water, to allay a burning thirst. After a long and unsuccessful search, I went deliberately to the beach and took a deep draught of the briny waves. Expecting that the chief would shortly return for me with a train of his followers, it occurred to me that I might secrete myself, though there was nothing certain to be gained by it, if I were successful, of which the probability was not great. With this object in view, I walked along close on the water's edge, that my footprints might be obliterated by the waves. After proceeding in this way for some distance, I left the shore, and started towards the interior, in quest of a place where I might dig a hole in the earth and cover myself with grass and bushes. I had gone but a little way inland, when, on ascending a slight eminence, whom should I meet, face to face, but the old chief and another of my tormentors! So the scheme came to nothing; but after others more feasible had so dolefully miscarried, it was not in human nature to lay this disappointment very deeply to heart. I made as though I was glad to see the old fellow, though, could I then have had my will of the savages, they would have been safely anchored in the middle of the straits. I told him (Heaven forgive me!) I was looking for them. The chief responded to my greeting only by ordering me to mount his horse. I requested leave to stay a little longer, and was refused. I again requested to be taken to Port Famine;—no, I should be taken to "Holland."

I mounted behind him, and we travelled all day in the direction of Cape Virgin. For two days and nights I had eaten nothing, and drunk nothing but sea-water,

and, in fact, had taken very little food for three days.
We arrived about dark at an eminence commanding a
view of their new squatting ground. Here we halted
to take a short survey of the encampment. To them,
doubtless, the prospect was beautiful; to me it was
heart-sickening, but I strove to keep up cheerful appearances. Down in a valley or deep marshy hollow,
covered with tall grass or rushes, an almost innumerable
drove of horses were seen grazing; and beyond, at a
short distance, the surface was thickly dotted with huts,
erected, or in process of erection, by female architects.
Children, in swarms like summer flies, and with no
more artificial covering than those insects, were capering
and shouting in high glee. At length we descended to
the rude village; after tacking about first to the right
and then to the left, like a ship against a head wind, we
came gallantly into town, and drew up at the chief's
lodge. I was glad to dismount, sore with bestriding the
skeleton of a horse.

Here I again took the liberty of proposing a trip to
Port Famine, offering to go alone, if they would not go
with me. The chief told me, with emphasis, to say no
more about it. He would take me to "Holland," and
there get rum and tobacco. "Only get me there," I
said to myself, "and much good may your rum and
tobacco do your old carcass!"

On the third day of our encampment here the tribe
was divided, and I was sent off with one of the chief's
lieutenants. A more bloodthirsty rascal could not be
found in the tribe. This step was probably taken by
the chief to get rid of my importunities to visit Port
Famine, the frequent renewal of which had evidently
worried him. My new guardian regaled my ears, from
time to time, with stories of his murderous exploits,
most likely in order to instil into me a wholesome
dread of his power, and a submissive temper under his
authority. The details of his bloody yarns are too
shocking to repeat. One story, on which he seemed to

dwell with peculiar satisfaction, as it was confirmed by more reliable authority afterwards, I will here relate, with such other particulars as I gained by subsequent information.

About two years before, the British brig Avon was in the Santa Cruz river. Captain Eaton, her commander, went on shore with his men, and bought some horses of the Indians, which he paid for in rum, tobacco, and trinkets. After receiving their pay, they played the same trick as with me,—refused to deliver the horses. The captain was about getting under weigh, when the Indians, perceiving his intention to leave them, went down to the shore opposite the vessel, and beckoned him to come on shore, signifying that they would give up the horses as agreed. The boat was sent ashore, and six or eight Indians returned in it to the brig. They surrounded the captain on the quarter-deck, and told him the horses were coming. He stepped to the rail with his glass, to observe motions on shore; while thus engaged, the savages came up behind, drew out their long knives, and stabbed him to the heart. He sunk lifeless on the rail, and fell upon the deck. Seizing him by the hair, and raising him partly on their knees, they cut his throat, and stabbed him again and again, to make the work of death sure. They then rushed upon the mate and stabbed him, but not mortally; he threw himself exhausted down the hatchway, and had just strength enough to secrete himself among the cargo. The boy was dealt with in the same manner as the captain, and one or two sailors, being wounded, succeeded, like the mate, in getting below deck and secreting themselves. The remainder of the crew were fortunately off in a boat at this time, and escaped the massacre. The savages ate and drank on board, and then plundered the brig of such articles as suited their fancy. Mr. Douglass, of " Holland," being on board the brig, was not murdered, but carried on shore and detained. A gentleman named Simms afterwards endeavoured to effect the release of Mr. Douglass. He gave them all that they demanded as ransom, and was then himself detained to keep his friend company. A third embassy was undertaken by Mr. John Hall, of whom the reader will learn more hereafter. He paid a large ransom for his two friends, and was then served as they had been. He succeeded in effecting his escape the next day; but Douglass and Simms were carried off, murdered, and, it is supposed—I believe with good reason—that their bodies were eaten. The Avon, after being plundered, fell into the hands of the remainder of the crew, and sailed for Montevideo.

I travelled with this ruffian about ten days. He was a hard master, though I cannot charge him with personal ill-treatment that amounted to cruelty. Our life was monotonous enough. We slept a good share of the time when we rested, drank pure water when we could get it, and ate what fell in our way; though the reader may be assured that we saw some hungry days. At the expiration of ten days, the tribe was reunited at a place agreed upon. Here we continued several days, the natives occupied exclusively with gambling, which was alike their daily labour and recreation. When the demands of hunger became too imperative to be longer postponed, they would go out and hunt, after which they resumed their games.

Gambling is a vice to which they are greatly addicted, and they pursue it with a perseverance and ardour worthy of amateurs in more civilized communities. The implements used are bits of guanaco-skin, about the size of common playing-cards, on which are rudely depicted dogs and a variety of other beasts, with divers mystic marks and scrawls, done with a stick in a pigment composed of clay, blood, and grease. Unlike their compeers in more enlightened circles, they put down stakes on only one side, for which the opposite players contend. In this way they rid themselves of their saddles, bridles, knives, and whatever other portable articles they may have to hazard. Nay, I have seen them inflamed to such a passion as to take the mantles from their women's shoulders, telling them to protect themselves from the cold as they could.

But where was "Holland" all this time? They told me at first that we should be only four days reaching it, and already more than ten had passed. On inquiry, they said that the journey would be completed in six days; on we went, for sixteen days more, with the same dull routine, the Indians assigning seven or eight days as the minimum time. The place seemed to be all the while receding. I had long since become aware that there was no truth in them; but persisted in questioning them, to call forth fresh lies, which they uttered with marvellous fluency, as if it were vastly easier than speaking the truth.

After the reunion of the tribe, I implored the old chief to take me back to his lodge, and to his especial care; to which he consented, much to my satisfaction. With him I felt a kind of security unknown elsewhere; under God, I relied alone on his protection. He alone of the tribe had the power to defend me, and I spared no pains to secure his good-will. To this end I made him large promises of such things as I thought would arouse his cupidity, or stimulate his appetites, as well as an abundance of ornaments for his wives and children, if he would only take me to some place inhabited by white people. This policy was extended to his household; disagreeable as the task was, I forced myself to caress his dirty children, and to tell them what pretty things I intended to give them. By these, and such-like demonstrations, I flattered myself it might be possible to keep on peaceable terms with old Parosilver, and enlist his authority for me, if circumstances should compel me to appeal to it.

The reunited tribe remained in camp three or four days, dividing their time between gambling and hunting. When I accompanied the hunters, as I sometimes did, I was sure to get something to eat towards night, as they invariably kindled a fire and cooked part of the game on the spot where it was killed. Their method of preparing all meats was essentially the same as has been described; tossing large pieces into the fire, or suspending them over it, till they were somewhat smoked and dried, and then devouring them, without salt, or any other condiment but the sauce of hunger. Cooking the ostrich, however, forms an exception : the feathers are plucked out, the bones dissected and removed; hot stones are placed within the body, the skin is tightly sewed together, and the whole is partially roasted on the embers. The lacings are then cut, and the meat is served up; it has an excellent flavour, far surpassing that of the domestic turkey. The bird is covered with a layer of fat, half an inch thick, which is melted, and collects in the body, forming a condiment which is relished as the greatest luxury of Patagonian living. If any fragments of the repast remain, they are slung to the backs of the saddles, and so carried home, dangling at the horses' sides, till they are so begrimed with dust as to defy all conjecture as to their quality or origin. These choice morsels are proffered to the home department, are received with smiles of gratitude, and devoured with a gust sharpened by long abstinence. It was noticeable that the plumage of the ostrich, though beautiful, was not at all valued by the Indians; large quantities of the feathers are blown all over the country, without attracting the least regard, while men and women disfigure themselves with paint, and load their persons with the cheapest of all trumpery, brass and copper, and beads, picked up from traders, or stolen.

The hunting of the guanaco is not only their chief reliance for food, but a spirited amusement, conducted after a fashion peculiar alike to hunters and hunted. Patagonia, as before mentioned, has no trees, but is covered here and there, in patches, with a kind of underbrush of scrub growth, and the plains extend back for hundreds of miles from the Atlantic shore, like a vast rolling prairie. This affords a clear and excellent hunting-ground, with nothing to conceal the game, or hinder the pursuer, except now and then a clump of low bushes, or the tall grass of the marshes. Two to four hundred Indians on horseback, bare-headed, and with their skin mantles about them, and each having the bolas and his long knife tucked beneath his belt, the whole followed by an innumerable pack of dogs of every kind, down to curs of low degree, make up a hunting party; as far as the eye can reach, their gigantic forms, diminished by the distance, may be seen projected on the horizon, their long hair streaming in the wind. Presently a thickness is perceived in the air, and a cloud of dust arises,—a sure indication that a herd of guanacos has been beaten up, and is now approaching. All eyes are fixed intently on the cloud; it soon appears as if several acres of earth were alive, and in rapid motion. There is a herd of from five hundred to a thousand of these animals, infuriated, rushing forward at their utmost speed, whatever direction they may chance to take, they follow in a straight line; and, as soon as their course is ascertained, the Indians may be seen running their horses at break-neck pace to plant themselves directly in the course of the living tide. As the game approach, the hunter puts spurs to his horse and rushes across their track. When within twenty or thirty yards, he jerks the bolas from his girdle, and, whirling it violently above his head, lets fly. The weapon usually strikes the head or neck of the animal, and winds itself about its fore-legs, bringing him to the ground. The hunter dismounts, cuts the victim's throat, remounts, and is again in pursuit. The whizzing missile, unerring in its aim, brings down another and another, till the party are satisfied with their chase and their prey. The dogs fall upon the poor animals, when help-lessly entangled by the bolas, and often cruelly mangle them before the hunter has time to despatch them.

Seldom does any one miss the game he marks. It is the height of manly ambition among them, the last result of their training, to excel in the chase.

` The sport being over, then comes the dressing of the meat. The body is split open, the entrails removed, the heart and large veins opened, to permit the blood to flow into the cavity. The Indians scoop up with their hands and eagerly drink the blood. When their thirst is satisfied, the remainder is poured into certain of the intestines selected for the purpose, to become—to their accommodating tastes—a luxury as highly prized as any surnamed of Bologna. The ribs are disjointed from the back-bone, and, with the head, discarded as worthless. The body is quartered, cutting through the skin; the quarters, tied together in pairs, are thrown across the horses' backs, and conveyed to the camp. Arrived at their wigwams, the chivalrous hunters never unlade their beasts, but lean upon the horses' necks till their wives come out and relieve them of the spoil. They then dismount, unsaddle their horses, and turn them loose.

Whilst remaining at our present encampment, strong indications of dissatisfaction were apparent, which manifestly had reference to me. There was a large party that had always entertained hostile feelings towards me; and I now found it necessary to exert myself to the utmost to quell their discontent, by making large promises of presents to men, women, and children, "due and payable" on arrival at some white settlement; also, by humouring their caprices, and flattering their vanity with the most honeyed words at my command. The reader, I hope, will not harshly judge of the deceptions which are here and elsewhere avowed in this narrative. I was placed in circumstances which, it seemed to me, made this a legitimate and necessary mode of self-defence. It was plain that my only way of escape would be by some negotiation for ransom, and the Indians had conceived expectations of very large profit to be made out of me. They were told, when we landed, that I was the captain of the ship,—an unfortunate error, but one that I could not repair. I was naturally looked upon as so much the more valuable hostage. My only resource was to act in character : to magnify my own importance, to increase their expectations, whenever I found myself sinking in the scale of their favour,—to make them feel, in short, that they had an immense interest in preserving my life, and getting me to "Holland," or some other white settlement, with the most convenient speed. And if some of the fictions appear gross, it is enough to say that they were such as seemed, at the time, to be adapted to the grossness of their apprehensions and desires, and to the most sure accomplishment of the purpose in view.

Yet, so false-hearted and treacherous were they, that one could never be for a moment certain what impression was made. Liars in grain themselves, it was only natural for them to distrust every one else. Whenever I spoke, and especially when making promises, the old chief would look me steadily in the eye, as though piercing my inmost thoughts. But, in process of time, I so schooled myself to the exercise, that I could return his look and tell the toughest stories without blinking. Some of them were to the full as credible as those of Munchausen. It was constantly necessary to put memory and imagination to the rack, to call forth something new and astonishing wherewith to divert their fancy, and preoccupy their minds from meditating mischief against me, of which I had continual reason to be afraid. Secure against any detection of the plagiarism, I drew largely from the adventures of Sinbad the Sailor, the marvels of the Arabian Nights, and the cunning devices of Gil Blas, the materials of which served, when duly mixed with my own veritable experience, to excite their curiosity, if not to awaken awe and superstitious reverence. They would sit around me for hours, as eager as so many children, their eyes and ears all intent, while in broken Spanish, mixed with a few

Indian phrases that had been grafted into my speech
through the ear, aided by abundant gesticulations, that
shadowed forth and illustrated whatever was obscure in
expression, I spun yarns of no common length, strength,
and elasticity. Sometimes, in response to a general
call from the company, the old chief, at the end of some
marvellous tale, would command me to tell it again.
This was no easy task, considering the freaks which my
imagination usually played, without restraint, in the
progress of the narrative. In no long time, however, I
learned to imitate the prudence of boys who turn down
the leaves of their books, or of Indians who break down
the shrubs and twigs along a new path, by taking special note of my deviations,—a sort of mental dog's-ear,
or way-mark, interposed at the point of departure. It
was not difficult to retrace the way at their bidding, and
give them the whole journey, to its minutest turnings.

The excitement and dissatisfaction which I had remarked and dreaded appeared to have died away, when
one night I had startling evidence that it was still
active. At the usual hour of rest, as I was expecting
every moment to be ordered, like a dog, to my cold
corner of the lodge, a gigantic, ill-favoured fellow made
his appearance, and exchanged, in an under tone, a few
words with the chief. Without comprehending a word
that was passing, I could see, by their significant
glances, that the colloquy concerned me, and that it
boded me no good. The giant soon disappeared. The
chief sat a moment in silence, rose, and ordered me to
follow him. To the question where he was taking me,
no other answer was vouchsafed than "Come along!"
We had proceeded but a short distance when I observed
a group of Indians sitting in a circle on the earth. The
sight almost froze my blood. The most dismal apprehensions seized upon me. There needed no wizard to
tell the import of the scene. The *fatal ring*, so much
to be dreaded by those who are cast upon the tender
mercies of savages, was set for me. The suddenness of

it aggravated the blow. It almost paralyzed thought, and arrested my power of motion. The catastrophe of the tragedy, I thought, is at hand, unless arrested by the interposition of a higher Power. In my way to the dreaded spot I sent up a silent supplication that He whose eye marked all my footsteps, and whose power was all-sufficient for my protection against utmost peril, would keep me in that hour of my "extremity," and make it, according to the proverb, His "opportunity."

Arrived at the ring, I found the Indians squatting on the ice and snow, awaiting us, with their cutlasses and large knives tucked under their blankets,—weapons they never carry except when they expect to use them. I was ordered within, and seated myself as near as possible to the chief. They presently began talking in rotation, as they sat, in their own tongue. Their words were mainly unintelligible; but the deadly malice that flashed from the eyes, kindled in the features, and animated the gesticulations, of some of them, left no room to doubt the significance of their speech. A part of them were clamorous against my life, as they had constantly been. Others appeared to be irresolute, and said little; but, so far as could be discovered, no voice was raised in my favour. The chief spoke last,—I hung upon his lips, and anxiously scrutinized his face and action. I gathered that he was in favour of holding on a while longer, and using me as a decoy, to lure others within their power; reminding them of my promises,—the quantities of rum and tobacco they were to get from me, the trinkets destined for women and children. He was for getting the booty before cutting the matter short with me. His remarks evidently had great weight with the council, and exerted a soothing effect on all of them. At this point I thought it a meet season to impress upon their minds that I was of some consequence in the world, and asked leave to speak for myself, which was granted. Thereupon I launched forth in an oration,

THE CAPTIVE ADDRESSING THE GIANTS.

the chief acting as interpreter, and retailing it to the circle sentence by sentence :

"Buenos Senores! Me mucho grande Americane capitan, mismo commodant mucho mass, mucha barca, mucha galeta, muchos soldados, muchos marinarios. Me tene mucho mucho big guns, bastante poquito mismo bastante, cutlass, pistols mucho bastante. Vuestros hombres, buenos per me, mi marinarios, mi soldados, buenos per vos. Othro corso usted malo rumpe me," &c. &c. &c. In such a jumble of Spanish, English, and Indian, duly set off with grimace and gesture, I gave them to understand that they were dealing with no inferior personage, but with one who was at home as good as the president; one having at command abundance of steamships and sailing vessels of all sorts, with soldiers and mariners, big guns and little guns, pistols, and cutlasses. That if they were good to me they would receive good from me and mine; but that, if they did me any harm, men would come from North America in numbers as incalculable as the hairs of their heads, and kill every mother's son of them. Furthermore, if they would take me to some white settlement, whether American, English, French, or Spanish, I would order the white people to give them rum, tobacco, flour, rice, sugar, and tea. *Of course* the white men could do no less than obey, and they would thus be enabled to indulge themselves in luxuries almost without limit.

It was evident, at a glance, that my speech was seasonable, and took effect in the right quarter. Their eyes stood out with wonder, and the sternness of their countenances was relaxed. They acquiesced in the proposal to postpone final action for the present, and see what could be made out of me before doing their worst. In a few days, they said, they would take me to " Holland;" but, no matter what time was limited, that " undiscovered country" seemed continually farther off, —"a name" without any "local habitation." Their conduct in this was determined, as I was afterwards assured, by the fact that they were entirely undecided what to do with me. They longed for the good things I had told them of, and their greedy appetites could only be satisfied by taking me to a white settlement. On the other hand, they were painfully suspicious that I meant to give them the slip, and dreaded the result of bringing me into the vicinity of any settlement; while, at the same time, my grandiloquent assumptions and lofty threats made them shrink from the thought of doing me serious harm. The big guns and little guns greatly disturbed their imaginations. In short, I seemed to them an ugly customer—bad to keep, and bad to get rid of. They temporized, therefore, promised and hesitated, and postponed, and promised again. There was no use in trying to hurry their movements. So I gave them line upon line, seeking every opportunity to deepen the troublesome impression that they assumed a mighty responsibility when they made me a prisoner, and that their welfare depended greatly on the issue.

CHAPTER IV.

THE next move of the tribe brought us within about a mile of Corey Inlet. The day after we halted, in full view of the South Atlantic, on looking out upon the water, two masts were plainly descried, evidently those of some vessel running down to this inlet. On going up an elevation commanding a better view, it proved to be a topsail schooner. She had undoubtedly mistaken this false cape for Cape Virgin, at the entrance of the Straits of Magellan. I pointed out the vessel to the Indians, and requested them to take me to the shore, that I might, if possible, communicate with her and be ransomed. After some delay, they complied; but, as e approached the beach, she was seen suddenly to haul off the shore and stand down the coast, having probably found out her mistake. We made all possible haste to gain the beach before she could have time to pass out of sight. I mounted a tall cliff, where I could distinctly see the men on deck, and, standing on the horse's back, waved my jacket, and made every possible demonstration to attract their notice. All in vain. The little vessel sailed steadily on, as if in mockery of my hopes. I watched her receding figure with an aching heart, till she vanished from sight. Thoughts of home and its familiar circle, of lost enjoyments, and of the suffering that must be a guest there, had long tantalized my sleeping and embittered my waking dreams. These were quickened and concentrated in a burning focus, by the light of such a vision from the world of my past existence, only to inflict the keener torture upon my sensibilities. My situation became more intolerable by every fresh disappointment. It was almost enough to drive me mad. Must I, then, give up all hope of rescue?

A few minutes passed, and the tempest of feeling passed with them. Reflection convinced me that the indulgence of such feelings was not only useless, but actually pernicious, as tending to unfit me for rational and successful contrivance. My condition truly was dreadful; so much the more necessary was it to exercise the most calm and patient and self-possessed prudence, in order to devise and execute any purpose of escape. Like the surgeon who looks with steady nerve on the quivering frame subjected to his knife, I must nerve myself to look the gloomy problem of my lot, without shrinking, fully in the face, and keep my emotions, in all circumstances, strictly under the control of the calculating judgment—a maxim, like many others, much easier uttered now than to be thought of then, and far easier asserted than exemplified. Fully bent on effecting my deliverance in some way, to the discovery of which all possible ingenuity was to be directed, my resolutions of self-control were heroic enough. But to fulfil them—to repress and disregard all those sympathies to which my whole being was bound—this was indeed labour, too great, I often feared, to be accomplished. When the stress of inward conflict oppressed me, I would spring from my crouching-place in the lodge, rush into the open air, and seize upon every object that could in any degree divert attention and divide my thoughts. These exertions, with God's blessing, sufficed to restore, in some tolerable measure, the mental equilibrium, and to rescue me from the dominion of feelings the unrestrained action of which would have driven me to madness.

During our stay of three or four days at this encampment, I had become so wearied with the monotony of their idleness, broken only by their desperate gambling, —the only thing, besides the chase, with which the Indians occupied themselves,—that for variety's sake, to divert my often-desponding moods, and to kill time, which hung heavily on my hands, I concluded to go out on a hunting frolic. Having procured a horse of the chief, and encased my lower extremities in a pair of native boots, much warmer than the ship shoes in which I had endured the cold, I set out with quite a party. We had gone six or eight miles, when I stopped for a short time, the rest of the troop riding off without regarding me. On remounting my charger, I put him to his utmost speed, in order to overtake them. While driving on at a furious rate, he stumbled and came to the ground, throwing his luckless rider over his head twenty feet or more, upon the hard, frozen ground. One ankle was severely sprained, and my whole body more or less bruised. So severe, indeed, was the shock, that I have occasional reminders of it to this day. No time was to be lost; and, with considerable effort and no little pain, I succeeded in remounting. The swelling of my foot soon made my borrowed boots extremely uncomfortable, and I wished myself safely back at the lodge; but, at whatever expense of suffering, I had no resource but to follow the hunters till such time as they should see fit to return. The remembrance of that day's torment will not soon be lost. We arrived at the camp late in the evening; and, having been unsuccessful in the chase, went supperless to bed. On crawling into the hut and removing my boots, a sad sight was disclosed; but there was no present remedy. Dragging myself wearily into my corner, I had just crouched upon the skin, which had served for a saddle during the day and was still reeking from the horse's back, when a great dog came along, and threw his whole weight upon the lame foot, causing me to scream aloud for the pain. I drew back the serviceable foot, and gave him a kick that sent him through the fire and against the front of the lodge. Sleep kept at a distance till near morning, when I gained a brief oblivion of suffering.

Day at last dawned, and with the morning's light came the busy note of preparation for removal. Down came the tents; the squaws packing up the furniture, and the Indians chasing and lassoing their horses. The noise and confusion, disagreeable enough under any circumstances, made the scene no inapt representative of chaos, from which I was glad to be delivered on the most expeditious terms possible; and I was easily persuaded to try my fortune again in the chase, more especially as we had nothing for breakfast. No words can do more than partial justice to one of these moving scenes. Not only the skin roofs of their wigwams, but the stakes and poles which constitute the frames, are carried along with them. Their furniture gives them little trouble, seldom consisting of more than the skins on which they sleep, an ox-horn tinderbox, a few sticks for roasting meat, and a leathern water-bucket. Tents and furniture are all packed together on their horses' backs. The pappooses in travelling are lashed to a kind of wooden sledge, rounded at the ends like sleigh-runners, and crossed with narrow slats, that bind the parts strongly together. The little brats are bound

upon these machines, which are so shaped that their
heads and feet are much below the general level of their
bodies,—a very uncomfortable position for the youngsters,
if they have as much sensibility to pain as other children,
of which I incline to doubt, as they are inured from birth
to almost every species of hardship. The sledge, with
its living burden, is thrown across the horse's back, and
made fast to the load. The mother mounts to the top
of the pack, resting her feet on the horse's neck, and
armed with a cudgel, with which she vigorously belabours
the beast, right and left. The pappooses, not liking the
quarters assigned to them, set up a general squalling.
Mothers and maiden aunts join in full chorus, drawling
out, at the top of their voices, "Hōrī! mutty, mutty!
Hōrī! mutty, mutty!" without the least change, to the
thousandth repetition. All these arrangements are made
with remarkable celerity—in thirty minutes not a tent
is left standing, but the whole tribe, their tenements and
chattels, wives and brats, are all packed upon horses, and
the motley cavalcade moves off like an army of beggars
on horseback.

On the present occasion the movement was delayed,
while we rode in search of something to eat. The chase
was unsuccessful, scarcely enough being obtained to more
than sharpen our appetites for dinner. The scanty meal
being over, the whole company began their journey,
which in its tortuous windings was not unlike that of
the Israelites in the wilderness, but unlike that in the
respect that we seemed to have no particular destination
or object, except to explore new hunting-grounds, and
gratify the capricious restlessness of the Indians. One
very desirable end was answered,—we got enough to
eat, as we were successful in killing a large quantity of
game. The Indians, it was noticeable, were never at a
loss to find their camps. So familiar did they seem
with all their haunts and the general shape of the country,
that though the surface presented to my eye scarcely any
distinguishable way-marks, they would strike off from

any point, however distant, and go with unerring aim straight to their tents. In returning laden with booty to our new homes, I was surprised to observe no indications whatever of water in the vicinity; a singular departure, at first sight, from their invariable custom, so far as I had noticed. Very soon the squaws issued from their huts, each with their leathern bucket. Curiosity prompted me to follow them a little way, when a spring was discovered, from which they had to dip the water with their ox-horn cups till the buckets were filled.

About this time a new phase of life presented itself, to cast light on an important item of the social economy established in Patagonia. Looking out of our wigwam one evening just at dusk, I noticed an unusual concourse of Indians about two hundred yards distant. There were fifty or more, headed by one of the most ruffianly rascals in the tribe, marching in the direction of our lodge. I spoke to the chief about it, whereupon he went immediately to the back of the hut, and sat down on his little bed, his cutlass hanging beside him from a knot of one of the stakes. This he took down, laid it across his knees, and folded his arms. Something, I saw, was wrong. In anticipation of the worst that might befall me, I had found, a short time before, the handle of an old knife among the chief's trumpery, and also an old blade; these I had put together, and the chief permitted me to carry it about my person, the only weapon he allowed me. I now planted myself on my knees beside him, and prepared to sell my life as dearly as possible, should the mob enter with evil designs towards me. The consciousness that I was in their power, and was sure to have the worst of any serious quarrel, made it my study to keep the peace with them as far as circumstances would admit; but there was a limit to my control of events, a very narrow limit, which I had constant reason to fear would be overborne by the impetuous hatred of my enemies, when nothing would be left but desperate resistance. Such a crisis seemed near, when the chief was himself reduced to a defensive attitude, and was indeed besieged in his own lodge.

The motley throng surrounded the hut, their numbers constantly swelled by fresh arrivals; some were squat upon the ground, others peeping through the crevices. Presently one of the number addressed the chief, and the two conversed for some time in a low and unintelligible, but decided and emphatic tone. The crowd outside appeared to be a good deal excited, and kept up a continuous hum of rapid conversation. I looked and listened, with mingled curiosity and dread, while the chief repeated the same thing over and over again, in a firm, authoritative tone, tinged with anger. Unable to conjecture what was on foot, or to bear any longer the agony of suspense, I patted him familiarly on his naked breast, told him he had " a good heart," begged that he would not suffer the Indians to harm me. " You go sleep," was his answer; " no Indians come into this house to-night." I inquired what they were after, but no answer was vouchsafed, and he resumed his mysterious colloquy with the outsiders. The idea of sleeping under such circumstances was out of the question; I was wide awake, and bent on keeping so,—sorely bewildered at the strange goings on, and not a little terrified, but holding fast by my sole weapon of defence, and waiting a favourable opportunity to interpose another inquiry. The chief turned his head; and, perceiving my vigilance, repeated in an angry tone his injunction to sleep. This was a drop too much; and, clasping my arms about his dirty neck, patting his breast, and looking (with as confiding an air as I could assume) into his dull eyes, I begged him to speak to me, to tell me what these men wanted. " Do they want to break my head?"

" The men don't want to hurt you," he said; "Indian wants a girl for his wife; poor Indian, very poor, got no horses nor anything else. I wont give him the woman."

So speedy a descent from the height of my fears was

not satisfactory; it was impossible to credit this explanation of such a formidable scene. I apprehended that
it was a pure fiction, extemporized for the purpose of
quieting me; but, as he seemed more communicative, I
swallowed my doubts, and questioned him further.
" What does poor Indian say ?"

" Says he'll steal plenty horses when we get where
they are, and give the woman plenty of grease. Says
he is a good hunter, good thief."

These high titles to consideration did not seem to be
admitted by the party they were offered to conciliate;
on the contrary, the chief pronounced him a sleepy
mink-skin of a fellow,—no thief at all ; one that would
never own a horse in the world. This opinion, which
he was good enough to favour me with, he communicated to the party chiefly concerned, telling him that
he was a poor, good-for-nothing Indian, he should not
have the woman, and that was the end of it. After a
little more jabber, and abundance of wrangling, the mob
dispersed, much to my relief. Satisfied, by further conversation on the subject with old Parosilver, whose
triumph over the mutiny had put him into better
temper than usual, that the affair did not imminently
concern my safety or welfare, I lay down to rest.

In answer to further inquiries,—for I must plead
guilty to a good deal of curiosity in respect of the poor
Indian and his blasted hopes,—I was informed that
without the chief's consent no marriage was permitted;
that, in his judgment, no Indian who was not an accomplished rogue,—particularly in the horse-stealing line,—
an expert hunter, able to provide plenty of meat and
grease, was fit to have a wife on any terms. He never
gave his consent for such lazy ones to take an extra
rib; but, he very considerately added, all the difference
it made was that some one else had to support the squaw
till her suitor proved himself worthy, and acquired sufficient wealth to justify taking her to his wigwam; and,
if he cared much for his *coury*, he would not be long in

earning her; it would make him a first-rate thief,—
the most indispensable title to favour in the tribe. It
appeared that the possession of two horses, one for himself and one for his intended, was regarded as the proper
outfit in a matrimonial adventure.

The women are somewhat given to quarrelling among
themselves ; and, when their " combativeness " is once
active, they fight like tigers. Jealousy is a frequent
occasion. If a squaw suspects her liege lord of undue
familiarity with a rival, she darts upon the fair enchan-
tress with the fury of a wild beast; then ensues such a
pounding, scratching, and hair-pulling, as beggars description. The gay deceiver, if taken by surprise, slips
quietly out, and stands at a safe distance to watch the
progress of the combat, generally chuckling at the fun
with great complacency. A crowd gathers round to
cheer on the rivals ; and the rickety wigwam, under the
effect of the squall within, creaks and shivers like a ship
in the wind's eye.

While the *contract* of marriage is so jealously regarded
by the chief as to be subject to a veto in every case
where a proposed match appears in his eyes unsuitable,
the *ceremony* is literally nothing at all. Due sanction
having been given by the supreme authority, the bride-
groom takes home his bride for better or worse, without
any of the festivity which graces similar occasions elsewhere. About this time,—for, as I had no means of
journalizing my experience, or even keeping the reckon-
ing of weeks and months, it is quite impossible to assign
dates,—a matrimonial transaction took place, accompanied by unusual solemnities. The rank of one party,
and the extraordinary accessories of the occasion, will
justify a particular notice of this " marriage in high
life."

One evening, the chief, his four wives, two daughters,
an infant granddaughter, and myself, were scattered
about the lodge, enveloped in a smoke of unusual
strength and density. While the others sat around as

unconcerned as so many pieces of bacon, I lay flat, with
my face close to the ground, and my head covered with
a piece of guanaco-skin, the only position in which it
was possible to gain any relief from the stifling fumiga-
tion. While in this attitude, I fancied I heard the
tramp of many feet without, and a confused muttering,
as if a multitude of Indians were talking together.
Presently a hoarse voice sounded in front, evidently
aimed at the ears of some one within, to which the
chief promptly replied. I caught a few words,—enough
to satisfy me that I was not the subject of their colloquy,
but that there was a lady in the case,—and listened
curiously, without any of the fright which grew out of
the previous negotiations. The conversation grew animated, and the equanimity of his high mightiness the
chief was somewhat disturbed. I cast a penetrating
glance into the smoke at the female members of our
household, to discern, if possible, whether any one of
them was specially interested. One look was sufficient,
the chief's daughter (who, by the way, was a *quasi* widow,
with one hopeful scion springing up by her side) sat
listening to the conversation, with anxiety and apprehension visible in every feature. Her mother sat near
her, her chin resting upon her hand, with an anxious
and thoughtful expression of countenance. The invisible
speaker without, it soon appeared, was an unsuccessful
suitor of the daughter, and had come with his friends to
press his claim. He urged his suit, if not with classic,
with " earnest" eloquence, but with success ill propor-
tioned to his efforts. The chief told him he was a poor,
good-for-nothing fellow, had no horses, and was unfit to
be his son-in-law, or any one else's. The outsider was
not to be so easily put off : he pressed his suit with
fresh energy, affirming that his deficiency of horses was
from want of opportunity, not from lack of will or
ability to appropriate the first that came within his
reach. On the contrary, he claimed to be as ingenious
and accomplished a thief as ever swung a lasso, or ran

off a horse, and a mighty hunter besides, whose wife
would never suffer for want of grease. The inexorable
chief hereat got considerably excited, told him he was
a poor devil, and might be off with himself; he wouldn't
talk any more about it.

The suppliant, as a last resort, appealed to the fair
one herself, begging her to smile on his suit, and assuring
her, with marked emphasis, that, if successful in his as-
pirations, he would give her *plenty of grease*. At this
last argument she was unable to resist any longer, but
entreated her father to sanction their union. But the
hard-hearted parent, not at all mollified by this appeal
from his decision to an inferior tribunal, broke out in a
towering passion, and poured forth a torrent of abuse.
The mother here interposed, and besought him not to
be angry with the young folks, but to deal more gently
and considerately with them. She even hinted that he
might have done injustice to the young man. He might
turn out a smarter man than he had credit for. He
might—who knew?—make a fine chief yet, possess
plenty of horses, and prove a highly eligible match for
their daughter. The old fellow had been (for him)
quite moderate, but this was too much. His rage
completely mastered him. He rose up, seized the
pappoose's cradle, and hurled it violently out of doors,
and the other chattels appertaining to his daughter
went after it in rapid succession. He then ordered her
to follow her goods *instanter*, with which benediction
she departed, responding with a smile of satisfaction,
doubtless anticipating the promised luxuries of her new
home, the vision of which, through the present tempest,
fortified her mind against its worst perils. Leaving the
lodge, she gathered up her scattered effects, and accompanied by her mother, the bridal party disappeared.

The chief sat on his horse-skin couch, his legs crossed
partly under him, looking sour enough. Presently the
bride and her mother returned, and now began the second
scene. The chief no sooner recognised them than a

sound—something between a grunt and a growl, but much nearer the latter than the former, and in a decided *crescendo*—gave warning of a fresh eruption. The rumbling grew more emphatic, and suddenly his fury burst on the head of his wife. Seizing her by the hair, he hurled her violently to the ground, and beat her with his clenched fists till I thought he would break every bone in her body, and reduce her substance to a jelly. Perhaps I was a little hard-hearted, but she had been one of my bitterest enemies, and I had a feeling that if some of her ill-will to me could be beaten out of her, I could be easily resigned to her fate. The drubbing ended, she rose and muttered something he did not like. He replied by a violent blow on the side of her head, that sent her staggering to the further end of the hut. This last argument was decisive, and she kept her huge mouth closed for the night. There was a silent pause for some minutes, and without another word, we ranged ourselves for repose. I thought the old heathen's conscience troubled him through the night; his sleep was broken, and he appeared very restless. Early the next morning he went to the lodge of the newly-married pair, and had a long chat with them. They thought him rather severe upon them at first; but after a good deal of diplomacy, a better understanding was brought about. The young people could hardly get over a sense of the indignities they had received; but in the course of the day they returned, bag and baggage, to the old chief's tent, and made it their permanent abode.

We now moved in a westerly direction, and on the way succeeded in capturing a good deal of game. Their mode of dealing with the carcass of the guanaco is enough to dissipate whatever appetizing qualities the meat—in itself very palatable—would otherwise possess. It was no uncommon circumstance, while the squaws were removing the hide, to see the dogs tugging at the other extremity, the women, meantime, crying out "Eh! Ah!" in a dissuasive, though not angry, tone. If the animals become too audacious, the ire of their mistresses is kindled, and they break out with "Cashuran cashahy!" a phrase equivalent to that which, in English, directs its object to a region unmentionable in ears polite.

The Indians have, strictly speaking, no profane expressions. I never could learn that they worshipped or had any idea of a Supreme Being. The only observance which bore any aspect of religion was associated with something we should little think of as an object of adoration—the tobacco-pipe;—though, how far this is, in fact, an object of idolatry in Christian lands, it might not become me to speculate. The only occasions on which the Indians discovered any appearance of devotion were those of smoking. This may have been only a symptom of intoxication, but the reader may judge for himself.

A group of a dozen or more assemble,—sometimes in a wigwam, sometimes in the open air. A vessel made of a piece of hide bent into a saucer-shape while green and afterwards hardened, or sometimes an ox-horn, filled with water, is set on the ground. A stone pipe is filled with the scrapings of a wood resembling yellow ebony, mixed with finely-cut tobacco. The company then lay themselves in a circle flat on their faces, their mantles drawn up to the tops of their heads. The pipe is lighted. One takes it into his mouth and inhales as much smoke as he can swallow; the others take it in succession, till all have become satisfied. By the time the second smoker is fully charged, the first begins a series of groanings and gruntings, with a slight trembling of the head, the smoke slowly oozing out at the nostrils. The groaning soon becomes general, and waxes louder, till it swells into a hideous howling, enough to frighten man or beast. The noise gradually dies away. They remain a short time in profound silence, and each imbibes a draught of water. Then succeeds another interval of silence, observed with the most profound and devotional gravity. All at length arise, and slowly disperse. Now, this may or may not have been a form of worship; but the circumstances attending it, the numbers uniformly engaged in it, the formality with which it was invariably conducted, the solemnity of visage, the reverential grimace, the prostration, the silence, the trembling,—these, and traits of expression which are more easily discerned and remembered than described, gave me a decided impression that the whole had a superstitious meaning. The natural operation of the tobacco, and of the substance mixed with it, might explain part of the symptoms,—the writhing and groaning,—but these appeared to be a good deal in excess, and there were other features of the case which appeared to require another solution.

I never asked any explanation. The mystery which savage tribes are so apt to throw around their religious rites, and their resentment at any unhallowed curiosity, I was not inclined to meddle with or provoke. If my conjectures were just as to the nature of this ceremony, inquiry might lead to unpleasant consequences. Ignorance appeared, on the whole, safer than knowledge of good or evil, gained at the risk of being caught trespassing on things forbidden. If any one thinks my precaution excessive, he is at liberty to take a different course whenever he finds himself in the jurisdiction of Parosilver, or any other Patagonian chief.

The inquiry may arise, especially in the mind of the religious reader, whether I attempted to impart to my captors any knowledge of God, his attributes and laws. The answer is quite ready,—No, and for a variety of reasons. The writer did not understand enough of either Spanish or Indian to communicate intelligible ideas on any matters beyond the range of the senses; and Patagonia is pretty barren of sensible phenomena, which made my stock of words more limited than it might have been under nore favourable circumstances. There was no finding "tongues in trees," or "books in the running brooks;" the land possesses neither in num-

bers sufficient to be converaable. "Sermons in stones,"
even, must have been of very pebbly dimensions, and
of no great weight. Had this difficulty been removed, I
confess I had no great desire to surmount it. I was the
object of suspicion and hostility. My life was in constant danger. To diminish, as far as possible, the
causes of dislike, to mitigate their ferocious hate, to
elude occasions of mischief, to delay what I feared could
not be very long prevented, was my continual study. If
the reader is not satisfied with this account of my conduct,
I am sorry for it, but cannot afford any words of contri-
tion. It is vastly easier, I may hint to the objector, to
prescribe another's duties, than to judge of one's own,
especially where the two parties are in circumstances so
widely differing. The Patagonians need the gospel—
and the law—as much as any people I could name from
personal observation. There was no trace of instruction
imparted at a previous period, and the reception Christianity would meet with among them is yet to be discovered.

Their pipes are made of a hard red stone, the bowl
dug out with whatever iron or steel implement is at
command to the dimensions of an ordinary clay pipe,
the stem about an inch square, and three inches long,
with a small perforation. A copper or brass tube,
about two inches long, is fitted to the stem, and serves
as a mouth-piece. This is made by bending or ham-
mering a metallic plate about a small round stick, and
soldering or cementing it with a glutinous substance
thickened with earth.

The copper, brass, and iron seen among them, was
probably procured from unfortunate vessels wrecked on
the coast. I was informed by Captain Morton that he
had touched at Sea Bear Bay for a harbour, and saw
there great quantities of iron pumps, ships' hanging
knees, and other gear, from wrecks of vessels of all sizes.
As he was bound for the land of gold, he thought it
scarcely worth his while to collect the baser metals.

Had he been homeward bound, he might have obtained a valuable cargo.

As ornaments, bits of brass and copper, of silver and German silver, have a high value among the Indians, and when the metals are plenty such adornment is very common. The children's shoes have small oval pieces sewed on in front, and they appear on other parts of their dress. When scarce, they are more seldom seen. Blacksmithing in Patagonia is something of the rudest. Two hard flat stones do duty, the one as anvil, and the other as hammer. Of the effect of heat in making the metals malleable, and of the art of tempering, the people have no knowledge. To make a knife, they take a piece of iron hoop, or iron in any practicable shape, and hammer away upon it at a provokingly slow rate. Their blows are not heavy enough to do much execution; but they keep up a constant tap, tap, tap, hour by hour, till the iron is flattened to the required shape and dimensions. It is then rubbed on a smooth stone till it is worn down to an edge, and finally inserted into a wooden handle. Sometimes melted lead is poured into the handle, but lead appeared to be a scarce commodity. All mechanic arts, if they deserve the name, are in an equally rude and primitive stage. The simplicity of these people's ideas is indeed extraordinary. In invention or constructiveness they are babes. A Yankee boy, six years old, would be a prodigy among them,—a miracle of genius.

An opportunity was afforded, while in camp, to see some specimens of their tailoring or mantua-making achievements;—either term is appropriate, as the male and female dress do not differ in form, and but slightly in the mode of adjustment. The mantle or blanket is worn around the shoulders; those of the women are fastened together by the corners under the chin with a stick for a pen; the men hold theirs around them with their hands, except that when hunting they tie a string around the waist.

The skins of young guanacos are selected for mantles, on account of the superior fineness and softness of the hair. Nearly a dozen skins are used for a single mantle, as a large part of each is esteemed unfit for use, and thrown away. The skins, while green, are stretched to their utmost tension on the ground to dry. When partially dried, they are scraped on the inside with a stone sharpened like a gun-flint, sprinkling the while with water, to facilitate the operation. When the surface is made tolerably smooth, and of a pretty uniform thickness, it is actively scoured with a coarse-grained stone, till it has a bright polish. The skin is again dried, then crumpled and twisted in the hands till it becomes perfectly soft and pliable. The thread, as has been stated, is made from the sinews of the ostrich. These are extracted by the exertion of great strength, and divided into strings about the size of ordinary shoe-thread. They are then twisted, the ends are scraped to a point, and when dry become stiff; they are now ready for use.

Two pieces of skin are cut to fit each other. The tailoress (for all the work, from the curing of the skins to the last results, is done by the squaws) holds the edges together with the left hand, and drills them for sewing with a sharpened nail, held between the first two fingers of the right hand; the pointed thread, held between the finger and thumb, is inserted and drawn through, and so the work goes on. The stitches are tolerably fine, and a very neat seam is made. Other pieces are added, and when the whole is finished the seams are rubbed smooth with a bone. The fur being worn inside, there remains the work of outside decoration. With a due quantity of clay, blood, charcoal, and grease, amalgamated for the purpose, the artist arms herself with a stick for a brush, and executes divers figures in black, on a red ground; which, if intended to shadow forth men, require a vigorous imagination to detect the purpose. They might pass for unhappy ghosts (if a little more ethereal in composition), or for deformed trees. They bear a rude resemblance to a chair in profile, or a figure 4; and are thickly disposed over the whole surface, in the attitude sometimes vulgarly termed "spoon-fashion." The garment is now complete; the edges are carefully trimmed with a knife, and the fabric is thrown over the shoulders, with the infallible certainty of fitting as closely as the native tastes require. There is no trial of patience in smoothing obstinate wrinkles. A "genteel fit" is the easiest thing in the world; wherein Patagonian tailors have decidedly the advantage of their fellow-craftsmen in civilized lands.

CHAPTER V.

AT our next halt we encamped in a deep, swampy valley. The weather was cold and stormy; rain, snow, sleet, and hail, fell alternately, but did not accumulate on the earth to any considerable depth. Fitful gusts of wind came sweeping through the camp, making the wigwams shake fearfully. Our old lodge gallantly rode out the gale; but, either owing to its straining and working in the storm, or to some defects in the original structure, leaked shockingly all night. I was repeatedly awakened by a stream of cold water running under me. Giving the skin roof a few knocks to lighten it of its watery burden, and shaking the wet skin which constituted my couch, I would throw myself down, and resign myself to repose; but before quiet was fairly restored, another inundation would drive me to my feet. The night wore away with me, wet, cold, and sleepless. After daybreak I rose, and continued for two hours in vigorous exercise to restore warmth to my chilled frame, before the Indians were astir. Fires were then kindled, and matters began to assume a more cheerful appearance.

The weather, quite cool on my first landing, had grown gradually colder, and was becoming inclement. I was scantily prepared to endure the severity of winter. My under-garments, as before related, were desperately expended in trying to signal passing vessels. Cravat and pocket-handkerchief were appropriated to the adornment of the women in our household, to the no small envy of less favoured ones. My sole article of linen was in shreds, and of a colour that would afford matter for speculation to a jury of washerwomen. Stockings and shoes were sadly dilapidated; coat and trousers were glazed with dirt and grease till they shone like a glass bottle. The contents of my pockets were all confiscated, —purse, keys, knife, &c.—and a pair of pistols, of the use of which my captors knew nothing, were taken to pieces, and the brass mountings suspended about the necks of the chief's wives. In short, my outer man was nigh unto perishing, and I had no visible resources to arrest or repair the process of time, while I was not sufficiently inured to the climate to adopt the native dress without serious risk to health. But none of these things were allowed to trouble me. I took no thought for the morrow, but, according to the scriptural injunction, suffered the morrow to take care for the things of itself, esteeming sufficient unto each day the evil thereof.

At an early period of my captivity, the chief and some other Indians had cast a longing eye on my clothes, and tried to seduce me into parting with them. They offered no compulsion in the matter, but resorted to all manner of tricks. It seemed that they thought a white man could afford to go without dressing. I explained to them that, having always worn clothes—having in infancy, even, unlike Patagonian piccaninnies, been externally protected against the fresh air—it was quite impossible for me to change my habits without the hazard of my life; and, if I should die in consequence of yielding to their wishes, they were reminded they would lose the valuable ransom they expected for me. This reasoning proved convincing; greatly as they longed for my wardrobe, they more desired rum and tobacco, and I was permitted the undisturbed enjoyment of the scanty covering left me.

The storm continued for two days and nights; on the third day it cleared up. About midday, observing a crowd of Indians together with a huge jargon of tongues, I learned, on inquiry, that a horse was to be killed; a matter which, it appeared, was always the occasion of a solemn powwow. On reaching the spot, a poor old beast, lean and lank, with a lariat about his neck, stood surrounded by some fifty Indians. The squaws were singing, in stentorian tones, "Ye! Ye! Yup! Yup! Lar, lapuly, yapuly!" with a repetition that became unendurable, and drove me to a respectful distance. The horse's fore-legs were fast bound together, a violent push forward threw him heavily to the ground, and he was speedily despatched with a knife; anticipating, by a few days, the ordinary course of nature. Soon after my return to the wigwam, a huge portion of the carcass was sent to our quarters and hung up, to furnish our next meals! After being duly dressed by the women, with the aid of the dogs, and scorched and smoked according to usage, it was served up,—my only alternative to starvation. Famine has no scruples of delicacy; if the reader is disgusted, he is in a state of sympathy with the writer.

Early the next day we (literally) pulled up stakes, and were on the move; and, after journeying all day, encamped in a situation very like the one we left in the morning. The Indians spent their time, as usual, in gambling and in combing each other's hair, with a brush made of stiff dry roots, tied up together. The operator received as a fee the *game* captured in the process. The reader will excuse a more explicit statement of what, though less abominable than cannibalism, is hardly less repulsive.

One evening our family circle were seated round a
fire, which sent up volumes of smoke sufficiently dense
to suit a savage of the most exacting taste, and which
drove me, as usual, to the back part of the hut, where
I lay flat on my face.   One of the chief's wives was in-
veighing against me, as was her wont, and a second
occasionally joined in the strain, by way of chorus.   A
third was cracking the bones of a guanaco, that her son
Cohanaco might eat the marrow.   The fourth and last
of the women was attending to a piece of meat for our
supper, fixed on a forked stick, in the smoke.   Two
sons were engaged, as usual, in doing nothing, except
occasionally begging a little of the marrow, and scrap-
ing their dirty legs with a sheath knife, by way of
diversion ; sundry by-plays and little pieces of mischief
served to fill up the spare minutes.   The old chief, who
had been silently regarding the scene, now commenced
talking, in a low, mumbling, guttural tone, to one of his
wives.   She was busily eyeing the toasting-fork, and
studying the process of cooking ; but, at her husband's
instance, left them, and drew from their repository of
tools a sharpened nail fixed in a wooden handle, like an
awl.   The chief stretched himself on the ground face
downwards : a surgical operation was plainly impend-
ing.   What could the matter be ?   Had the chief, in
the excess of his plumpness, burst open, like ripe fruit,
requiring to be sewed up ?   I drew my head from
beneath the protection I had provided against the
smoke, and rose on my knees, to get a better view.
The huge, black, greasy monster lay extended at his full
length ; his wife pinched up the skin on his back,
pierced it with her awl, and continued the process till a
number of perforations were made, from which the
blood oozed slowly.   I asked the meaning of this operation, and was told by the chief that he had pains in his
back, for which this was the best remedy.   Blood-
letting, it seemed, is no monopoly of the faculty.   I
told him that in my country we applied in such cases a

liquid called opodeldoc, an infallible remedy, and promised to procure him some when we got to Holland. This was henceforth added to my list of inducements.

The old fellow righted himself, and leaned against one of the pillars of his palace; one of his partners pulled up the toasting-fork, and jerked the half-roasted and more than sufficiently smoked meat upon the ground, seized the knife which the boys had been playing with, and cut the mess into liberal pieces, which were thrown broadcast on either side. The chief's appetite did not appear to be affected either by his indisposition or by the extraordinary remedy applied; his portion of the cárne disappeared behind his great white teeth with a haste that seemed to involve no waste.

Rheumatic affections, they told me, are very common among them; the chief showed me the arm of one of his wives, which was scarred from the wrist to the shoulder by the awl; and the operation was afterwards performed on other members of the family.

Again we took up the line of march, travelling, as near as I could judge, west-north-west, and killing a quantity of game, both guanaco and ostrich. But the hardship of my life, aggravated by a constant flesh diet, and that eaten half raw, and at irregular seasons,—often going two days without food,—had, by this time, brought on a dysentery. This was no more than I had expected; but I knew of no remedy, and had to endure it as I could. We encamped, on the second day, near the banks of the river Gallegos; a fine spring of water issued from the river-bank into a low marshy ground skirting the margin of the stream. By this time my illness had increased, till I felt unfit to travel farther, and began to think that death could not be distant. No change of diet was practicable, and there was nothing to counteract its effect on my system. The pain and weariness of travelling did their part to aggravate the disorder; and mental discouragement—the sickness of hope deferred—completed my prostration.

No human being in that desolate land cared for my
sufferings more than they would for those of a dog.
Worn out with the constant irritations of a state of
epistence odious to every sensibility, tired and dis-
heartened, but for one thought I could have gladly laid
myself down to die, to get at once and for ever beyond
the reach of my savage tormentors. The thought of
home, of wife and child, of friends and country, and all
the unutterable emotions that respond to these precious
names, at once tortured and strengthened me. These,
and the thought that perhaps, after patient endurance,
Divine Providence would restore me to the objects of
my famished affections, made life still dear. These
strengthened me to suffer and to strive.

As I crawled out of the lodge, to look upon the sun
and breathe the pure air, and be refreshed by breezes
untainted with the breath of cruel men, it came into my
mind that some palatable or even tolerable species of
plant or root would be wholesome for me. On looking
about, there presented itself a specimen of large dock,
such as is common in the United States—a weed of
humble pretensions, but why not worthy of a trial?
With what strength remained at command, I began a
process of "extracting roots," with good success.
Taking a quantity into the hut, and roasting them in
hot ashes, they were found to be not distasteful; I
filled my pockets with them, and abandoned flesh diet
for a little time, to the sensible though gradual relief of
my sufferings. Fortunately we had a season of bad
weather, which prevented any advance movement for
four or five days, and gave me time partially to recover
strength. I could not sooner have kept my seat on a
horse; and, if the alternative had been presented, the
Indians, as I very well knew, would sooner have
knocked me on the head than have allowed me to
hinder their march for a day. A powwow was held
over another horse, unserviceable alive, and therefore
marked for diet; but this time I did not compete for

any part of his carcass, my pocket-stores being quite sufficient and more attractive. But in the fate of the poor beast I read a warning to myself, to make haste and get well enough to move at the first signal.

Away again,—this time facing about, and passing down the river. I needed rest; but, at whatever expense of suffering, needs must when a certain old gentleman drives. At the next stopping-place my services were called into requisition in a new department. One forenoon, as I sauntered towards our wigwam, after a stroll among the smutty huts, to kill time and divert painful thoughts, I was hailed from within by the chief, "Arke, Beney!" On entering he appeared to be conversing, in low, gurgling sounds, with his lately-married daughter, who was running her hands through the shaggy hair of her young hope, as she talked. Something was plainly wrong in her youngster's top-knot, and some unpleasant task in relation thereto was as plainly about to be imposed upon me. The chief resolved my doubts, by ordering me to cut off a portion of the shag; I objected a want of the proper implements, but the mother silenced me by producing an old pair of scissors, in no condition to cut anything. Calling for a file, the rusty edges were brought into a tolerable state, and I approached the task. Such a sight! If the hair now would have obeyed a mesmeric pass, without the need of manual contact,—if the job could be performed with closed eyes, and insensible nostrils, and absent mind! Faugh! I hurried through the penance, hiding disgust, and assuming the appearance of good-will, and made good my escape into the fresh air. And so I must turn barber, and, in all likelihood, have the dirty heads of half the tribe put under my nose! What would come next?

Our next move took us across the river Gallegos, in shoal water, barely up to the horses' knees. The current was rapid and masses of floating ice were swept along with it. When halfway across, my horse took fright, reared, and, in attempting a sudden turn, precipitated me into the water, and fell heavily upon me. The ducking and the bruise together were severe, and, among other disasters, the crystal of my watch was broken by the shock. This I had kept carefully secreted, as a last resource, to amuse the savages when other expedients should fail,—when memory and invention could yield no more tales, when promises should have become threadbare with repetition, and when pretensions of greatness at home should have lost their power by the every-day disclosure of present weakness and humiliation.

We—that is to say, myself and the old horse—kicked and floundered a while in the cold water, till at last the creature succeeded in rising, and I followed his example. We waded ashore, dripping, amidst the uproarious laughter of the whole troop. Once more mounted on my Rosinante, we resumed our line of march. The chill from my cold bath so benumbed me that I had to dismount and lead the horse, to recover, by brisk walking, some portion of animal warmth. Our course was down the river towards the Atlantic. Being unsuccessful in the chase, we pitched our tents at night, supperless, and without prospect of breakfasting the next morning. A small fire was lighted, which I hugged as closely as possible, to thaw my stiffened limbs; and then, cold, wet, and hungry, fagged to extremity, cast myself on the ground, to repose as I might. The next morning was stormy. It cleared up in the afternoon, and the Indians sallied out to find some food. My only refreshment before their return was a little grease, which one of the squaws scooped out of an ostrich-skin with her dirty thumb and finger. It was so black that its pedigree—whether guanaco, ostrich, or skunk, or a compound gathered at random from beast and bird—was a problem defying solution; but famine is not fastidious, and I swallowed greedily what, a few months before, I should hardly have thought fit to grease shoes with. The men came back with a few ostriches and skunks. The chief received as his portion one of the quadrupeds. The associations connected with its name, as related to one sense, were not adapted to prepossess the others in its favour; but I made shift to do justice rather to the Indian than to my habitual tastes.

During the three days we remained here, the long-concealed watch was brought to light. The filth of the natives, the condition in which their huts and their persons were always suffered to remain, the swarms of vermin they housed, had imposed upon me extraordinary care to prevent the natural results upon my own person; but no amount of precaution was sufficient to avert them. The reader will excuse me from speaking more particularly on this head. Enough to say that I found myself intolerably tormented. The chief ordered an examination of the case, and sent for an Indian to deal with it according to their art. While divesting myself of my garments, one by one, for this purpose, the old fellow caught sight of the hidden treasure. I knew that it was useless to attempt any longer to retain it, and handed it over. He was vastly pleased with it. I wound it up, and put it to his ear. He was as delighted at the unexpected sound as a child with its first rattle. I explained its use in keeping the hours of the day, but he cared for nothing but the ticking. The breaking of the crystal was explained, and he was informed that another should be procured as soon as we reached ".Holland,"—another inducement, I hoped, to speed our passage there.

The inspection disclosed a state of the cuticle which would be thought dreadful in a civilized land. The chief, however, looked as calm as beseemed a surgical examiner, and in a good-natured guttural exchanged a few words with his assistant, who placed himself by my side, and fixing his eyes steadily upon me, begun swinging his hands and howling like a wild beast. The comparison was not far out of the way, for he gave a sudden spring,

fastened his teeth on my neck, and commenced sucking
the blood, growling all the while like a tiger! For a
moment I thought my hour had come. I weaned the
rascal as soon as possible, not knowing what his taste of
blood might come to, if too freely indulged. It seemed
like a refinement upon cannibalism, but was, in fact, as
I soon ascertained, the regular treatment made and provided by Patagonian science for the relief of severe
cutaneous affections.

The chief, all this while, recurred with undiminished
pleasure to the ticking of his new toy. When his
curiosity had at length abated, he returned it to me. I
wrapped it carefully in a rag, and enveloped it afterwards
in a young colt's skin provided for its reception, when,
by direction of its present august proprietor, it was suspended among other valuables from one of the stakes of
the hut, near the spot where his highness customarily
reposed. It was not, however, allowed long to remain
quiet. I was ordered to take it down and hold it to the
ears of all the visitors to the lodge. Forty times a day
it had to come down for this purpose, till I got so tired
of my showman's duty that I wished the watch in
the bottom of the sea. The Indians, as they listened
to its vibrations, would stand in every attitude of silent
amazement, their eyes dilated, their countenances lighted
up in every feature with delighted wonder, and then
break out in a roar of hoarse laughter, the tone of which
strangely contrasted with the infantile simplicity of their
demeanour. The business was dreadfully annoying, and
yet it was plain that a new and almost unbounded power
affecting my destiny was hidden in that little machine.
It had captivated the chief, and struck an awe over the
tribe like the rod of an enchanter. Whether it boded
good or evil, was another question.

Our next move took us in a west-north-west direction,
and in our progress we not only secured abundant game
of the ordinary varieties, but encountered and killed a
young lion,—to use the popular term,—the first living

specimen I had seen in the country. I had seen their
skins in possession of the Indians, and heard stories of
their chase. This was a youthful creature, about the
size of a well-grown calf of six weeks. I was riding
side by side with the chief across a piece of low bushy
land, when the dogs gave token that they scented
something uncommon. We halted, and the chief cried
out to the dogs, "Chew! Chew!" They were off in a
jiffey, rushing hither and thither through the bushes,
barking furiously, and soon drove the beast from his
covert. Other Indians, a little distance off, ascertaining
what was in the wind, made after the game with a
reinforcement of dogs. The chase began in good earnest.
Horses, riders, and dogs, from all points of the compass,
were scampering to the scene of action, hallooing, barking, howling, enough to frighten any unsophisticated
lion out of his senses. Some were running full tilt, to
cut off his retreat; while the hunters, bareheaded, leaning forward in their saddles and urging their horses to
their utmost speed, whirled the bolas about their heads
and let fly with a vengeance, with no other effect than
to arrest the furious animal, and cause him to turn in
desperation on the dogs, and drive them back yelping
with pain. Others of the pack, watching their opportunity, would spring upon his back and fasten their
teeth in his flesh. He brushed them off with a single
stroke of his paw, as if they had been flies, and was
again in motion, halting occasionally to give fight to his
nearest assailant. Now and then the bolas is hurled at
him, but his lithe limbs, though sometimes entangled,
are not fettered by it, and his prowess is hardly diminished. The Indians press around him; the battle
waxes fiercer; his whole strength is taxed. "Chew!
Chew!" roar the savages; the flagging dogs return
fresh to the onslaught, and, after a hard and unequal
contest, the animal is fairly overborne by numbers, and
despatched by the blows of the Indians. I had kept in
the vicinity, but yet at a respectful distance, and now

rode up to view the slain, amidst the howlings of the wounded dogs and the boisterous laughter of the hunters. It was a beautiful animal, with soft, sleek, silvery fur, tipped with black; the head having a general resemblance to that of a cat, the eye large and full, and sparkling with ferocity.

After the Indians had eyed their game sufficiently, and talked and laughed and grunted their satisfaction, and congratulated themselves generally on their victory, and severally on the part each had taken, the body was driven off on the back of a horse, and the hunters again spread themselves over the country. Some ostriches were soon started up. The chief drew out his bolas, put spurs to his horse, and darted away. His mantle fell from his shoulders; his long, straight black hair, so coarse that each particular hair stood independently on end, streamed in the wind; his hideously painted face and body loomed up with grotesque stateliness, and the deadly missile whirled franticly over his head. The whizzing weapon is suddenly hurled at his victim, the chief still sitting erect in his saddle to watch its effect. His horse suddenly stops,—he dismounts nimbly, seizes the entangled bird by the throat, and swings it violently around till its neck is broken. As I rode up he depoposited the great bird on my horse, remounted, and rushed in pursuit of another. That was killed and also placed in my keeping, making me a kind of store-ship. Others pursue the guanaco with equal success, till they are satisfied with their booty. We ride up to a convenient thicket, a fire is lighted, a portion of the prey is cooked and eaten, the remnants of the feast and the residue of the game are duly packed up, and the whole troop is under march for the camp.

CHAPTER VI.

THE chief occasionally made a speech to his subjects from the door of his lodge, wherein he invariably inculcated the duty of hunting industriously to procure meat, and a due supply of grease, for their families. He never had an auditor in sight, for his faithful lieges considered the speech from the throne a decided bore, and, if one happened to be passing, he was sure to dodge into the nearest hut till the infliction was over; but the leathern lungs of the orator could not fail to make him audible in many of the wigwams. In length his performances more resembled the official addresses of our republican rulers than those of his royal cousins of Europe, seldom falling short of a full hour. In style, they came nearer the proclamations of a crier. He would proceed in a monotonous rumble to the end of a sentence, and then defy contradiction by repeating several times, "Comole! comole! comole!" after which he paused as for a reply. No one having the audacity to take up his challenge, he would go on croaking the same things with tedious iteration. After listening very patiently to one of his harangues, I inwardly applauded the taste of his subjects in getting as far as possible out of the reach of his voice.

One forenoon, as I was beginning to feel impatient to move,—for every moment seemed to fan the flickering hope that we would soon reach a place affording some avenue of escape, and this restlessness always made camp-life doubly dismal,—the chief informed me that we should decamp that day. Preparations had commenced, when one of his daughters came in with a child crying at a tempestuous rate. The version which she gave of his complaints arrested the marching orders. A messenger was forthwith despatched for one skilled in the healing art. The physician soon arrived, armed.

F

with two small packages rolled up in pieces of skin,
about a foot long and three or four inches in diameter,
which I took to be his medicine-chest. He walked
gravely in, laid down the packages, and squatted beside
the mother, who held the little patient in her arms.
Whatever his ailment might have been, his lungs could
not have been impaired, for he was roaring like a young
buffalo. Not a word was spoken for some time, the
doctor all the while looking him very steadily in the
eye. Then came a sudden calm, importing that the
little fellow experienced some relief, or, more probably,
that he was exhausted. The doctor ordered an application,—not of hot water, according to the prescription
of Sangrado, but of a mortar made of clay. The clay
was brought, the anxious mother worked it over with
her two hands, spitting upon it to give it the requisite
moisture, and having reduced it to the consistency of
thick paint, bedaubed the little fellow from head to foot,
giving him a decidedly original appearance. He evidently took umbrage at this unction, and discoursed in
his shrillest tones till he was fairly out of breath. The
medicine-chests were opened, but, instead of medicinal
herbs, disclosed only a bunch of ostrich's sinews, and a
rattle eight or ten inches long. The physician commenced fingering the strings, and muttering almost
inaudibly. This lasted four or five minutes, at the
expiration of which he seized his rattle, and clattered
away furiously for a minute or two, and resumed his
place by his patient, eyeing him intently as before. He
then turned with an air of importance to the chief, who
had been crouching cross-legged on his couch, leaning
forward, with his arms tightly folded on his breast, and
watching anxiously the progress of the treatment. The
man of skill broke silence : "I think he is better, don't
you ?" The chief nodded, and grunted assent. The
same appeal was made to the mother, and received a like
response. Another plastering was ordered, another
burst of melody followed the application, the mysterious

strings were again fingered, duly followed by the rattle. The parent and grandparent once more assented to the leech that the child was better. The chief took out a piece of tobacco, and cut off enough for about two pipefuls, which was tendered and gratefully accepted as a professional fee. The strings were tied up and replaced in their proper receptacle, and the rattle was shaken with hearty good will, whether by way of finale to the cure, or as a note of gratitude for the fee, or of triumph for success, could not easily be guessed. But the practitioner had scarcely evacuated the lodge, before his patient broke out more vociferously than ever; which I thought would somewhat shake the faith of his guardians in the treatment he had received. But no; their confidence in their medical adviser was not to be blown away by a breath, or even a tempest. They evidently regarded him as nearly infallible. His remedies were obviously aimed more at the imaginations of his spectators than at the body of his patient, but it was no concern of mine. Patients among us have to endure more disagreeable applications than wet clay. The noisy brat became quiet, to our great relief. He shortly appeared to be quite well, and continued to thrive for some time, as I had opportunity to witness.

The tribe went ahead with alacrity, to make up for the loss of time this sickness occasioned. We moved off another day's journey towards nowhere in particular, and settled there at night. Then ensued another season of camp life, feasting and fasting, gambling and quarrelling, and venting superfluous wrath in an abundance of "Cashuran cashalys." The chief was slightly indisposed, and I amused him with a description of the manner in which our physicians count the pulse of their patients. He listened with considerable interest, and sat thoughtfully ruminating on the matter. He came to an unexpected and alarming conclusion; putting this and my story of the *opodeldoc* together, he made up his mind that I was a physician myself! I protested against this inference, fearing that no good would come of the responsibilities he was inclined to impose on me. But the disclaimer was useless,—he stuck to the opinion; and in no long time it was understood through all the tribe that I was a distinguished doctor.

Now, it came to pass, at this critical. turn of affairs, that a certain widow, of pretty ripe years for a Patagonian, was taken suddenly ill. Her husband had been murdered many years before, by one of the tribe. She was possessed of several horses, and, in virtue of this wealth, held an aristocratic position in society. A messenger brought the tidings to the chief, who ordered me forthwith to set the watch, and go with him to her residence. I again assured him I knew nothing of sickness or medicine. He told me he knew better, and bade me come along without delay. There was no resisting his will, and I armed myself accordingly with the "ticking machine," and followed my master on my first professional visit. On approaching the widow's lodge, our ears were greeted with a hideous clamour, which momentarily increased as we neared the spot. A great crowd of Indians, of both sexes, surrounded the wigwam, severally and collectively making the most villanous noise ever heard. The crowd was dense, both within and without, but gave way for the chief and the great foreign physician to enter. The first order I gave was to stop their singing, whereat there was a silence so blank that the fall of a pin would have been audible,—that is, if there had been a floor for it to fall upon. With what dignity I could command, I walked up to my patient. There she lay, crouched on a bit of horse's skin, so withered, shrivelled, and contracted, that it seemed as if a bushel-basket might have covered her, bed and all. I knelt by her side, drew forth the watch, grasped her by the wrist, and felt for her pulse. But, to my surprise, I could not feel it. I fussed and fumbled a long time, and finally arrived at the mortifying conclusion that I was so ignorant as not to know

the position of the artery! The patient was frightened
at so unprecedented a proceeding; but I succeeded in
quieting her fears, though not, alas! in counting her
pulse. However, it occurred to me that it was all one
whether I did or not ; so, keeping up an imperturbable
gravity becoming my office, I continued for some time
to look wisely at the watch, holding her wrist in profound
silence. When I judged that a due impression had
been produced on the awe-stricken spectators, I ventured to prescribe, not a clay plaster, for the patient
was dirty enough, in all conscience; nor yet any compound of drugs, for I had none to administer; and as
to roots and herbs, I durst not inflict upon her stomach
substances of unknown properties; but, after a little
thought, I ordered some water heated blood-warm, and
the patient to be washed, and thoroughly scrubbed from
head to foot. This, I thought, met the most obvious
indications of her case, as I doubt not a whole college
of physicians, upon a superficial view, would have unani-
mously agreed. There could not have been a doubt as
to the novelty of the prescription; the respectable relict,
it is safe to say, had never been washed so thoroughly
from infancy to that hour. Minute directions were
given for the bath, that the scrubbing should be particularly smart and thorough. She was, furthermore,
put upon a strict diet, excluding *grease* and all such
luxuries, and we slowly retired from the sick-room.

My solemnity was not affected,—far from it. Promo-
tion from barber and showman to the dignity of physician to the chief was too dangerous to be lightly
considered. In fact, anxiety drove sleep from my eyes,
and I fervently prayed for the recovery of the widow;
fearing, from what I knew of the superstitions of the
savages, that in case of her death I should be held
responsible. In this particular case, as very soon
appeared, I misjudged; but of the general principle I
had startling confirmation.

The widow was better,—my prescription worked to

a charm,—but her days were shortened. Late one night, after we had all retired to rest, a ferocious-looking rascal came into the chief's lodge; he muttered a few words to the chief, who arose, and went with him to the front of the wigwam. They conversed in a low tone several minutes, and separated, apparently with mutual satisfaction. I sounded the chief cautiously in reference to the matter in hand. Calmly, and without reserve, as if it were a very ordinary transaction, he said that the savages wished to kill the widow, in order to possess themselves of her horses, which they wanted to eat. I asked no further questions, being fully satisfied that he connived at the dark deed, which was consummated without delay. Before this tragic result, I had taken pains to disabuse the mind of the chief as to my supposed medical skill, and was able to relieve myself of the dangerous and burdensome honour.

Strange flesh was eaten by the Indians about this time; I was told it was *lion-meat*, but was not invited to partake of it. The same thing was observed several times; at times, too, when I was positive they had killed no wild animals without my knowledge, or which were not disposed of openly. The nature of my suspicions may be easily conjectured; yet I made no inquiries, in even the most casual manner, as to their disposition of their dead. It was painful to think of the atrocities, that were but too probably shrouded under the mystery they cast over these transactions. On one occasion, however, a young Indian, who could speak a few words of Spanish and English, told me that they had killed and eaten three men. Whether he meant to have me understand this as a singular case, or as a common action of the tribe, I do not know; I made no inquiries of him. In fact, the statement was volunteered by him; and so painful was the subject, that I left him abruptly, in the middle of a sentence.

We again moved in a north-westerly direction, taking a goodly quantity of game on the route, and settled in a wretched, marshy spot. The wind was high, and made the tents quiver like a ship in a gale; a storm set in, beating through the roofs, drenching and chilling me through all the night. On the evening of the second day of our encampment here, an incident occurred which fearfully confirmed the wisdom of my decision to renounce all title to medical skill. As I was seated by the dying embers of a little fire, surrounded by our motley household, and tugging manfully at a bit of half-raw meat, which constituted my evening meal, while a large piece was in process of cooking over the fire, we were suddenly startled by a cry of distress, followed by the distinct alarm of *murder*. The chief drew back to the rear of his lodge, took down his cutlass, and ordered me back from the fire, which was at once extinguished by two of his squaws, while the other two ran to the door, and set up a loud, lamentable wailing. All the women throughout the camp were, in like manner, giving their voices to the air, and "making night hideous;" and not a male Indian ventured to show his head for an hour more. It was to me an hour of fearful suspense, the agony of which I cannot describe. At last a man came and told the chief that a doctor had been murdered. He had visited a woman professionally, and treated her case with charms and spells, but his prescriptions effected no satisfactory result; and her husband went in a rage to his lodge, and stabbed him with repeated blows, to make the work of death more sure. It was a singular circumstance, that men capable of deliberate murder, and who had so recently, with the tacit or open sanction of the chief, strangled a woman for her horses, should have shown so much alarm at the cry of murder on this occasion. The victim was an enormously fat man, weighing, I should judge, nearly four hundred pounds. A horrible sight presented itself the next morning, on going out of our hut; the snow around the doctor's lodge was saturated with his blood. I drew back from the sickening spectacle, unable to

look upon it with composure. Beyond their exhibition
of stupid terror in the night, no notice was taken of the
act; and about noon the camp broke up. We travelled
till night, meeting with no success in the chase, and
encamped on an extensive plain, near a good spring of
water.

It was an occasional diversion to watch the children
at their sports, of which a favourite one was throwing
ostriches' feet, with the sinews of the legs attached.
The toes are cut off, and a pair of the feet are tied together, with a piece of sinew about a yard long. The
children begin to practise the sport as soon as they are
able to walk, and will continue the amusement all day;
one boy throwing them into the air, and others throwing
and hitting them as they fly, therein serving an appren-
ticeship to the grand manly accomplishment of hurling
the bolas. Young Cohanaco, the chief's youngest son,
appeared to excel all others; he was looked upon as a
remarkably smart and very active lad; and though he
was six or eight years old, was not yet weaned! All
the tribe fondled and caressed him; he would practise
with the boys, often without any covering to his back,
till excited and almost exhausted; then he would run
into the lodge, take refreshment at his mother's breast,
and speedily return to his sport.

All this time *Holland* was not forgotten, but the chief
and his lieges were continually reminded of the urgent
reasons for taking me there without delay; the presents
which could only be obtained there, the fearful consequences of suffering me to come to harm, the great ships
with the big guns, &c. &c., that would assuredly avenge
me upon the whole tribe,—with what effect, beyond allay-
ing present irritations and discontents that threatened
me, it was impossible to determine.

A novel sample of farriery offered itself to my observation one day, while hunting with the chief; my old
horse, on a sudden, began to hobble, and very nearly
cave out. I watched him some time, and jolted on,

suffering somewhat from his uneven movements, but could not discern the occasion of the difficulty. On dismounting and examining his feet, nothing serious was perceptible, except that the hoofs were worse for wear, and broomed up a little. I remounted, and gave the poor creature a smart drubbing, to overtake his owner, if possible, and consult him on the case, which was one wherein I was content to defer to his wiser judgment. Sufficient steam was raised to bring us abreast of the chief, who, on hearing what was the matter, put spurs to his horse, and told me to come on—" Bueno caballo, se campo, campo." I tried to comply, but it was hard starting the beast, though I used up considerable wood to that end. The chief having got far in advance, and finding me desperately in arrears, hove-to, and waited for me. I toiled on, and succeeded in working a passage to his position. He dismounted, inspected the horse's feet, and, directing me to wait his return, rode off. He soon reappeared with a piece of guanaco-skin, which he tied securely about the hoof of the lame foot. I expressed some surprise at this method of shoeing horses ; but he said, " Buenos zapatos,"—good shoes,—and the event confirmed his words. The lameness nearly disappeared, and we jogged on together without any further trouble.

While at this camping-ground, the chief one morning arose in a towering passion at some words let fall by one of his wives, and exhibited another sample of the rigour of matrimonial discipline, very similar to that which graced the nuptials of his daughter. He gave her a tremendous beating, which seemed enough to kill her outright ; but she took it very calmly, as a sort of necessary evil incident to the married state.

Once more on the move, the squaws taking charge of the furniture and baggage, including the pappooses, and the men riding in advance as usual, to chase supplies for the larder. Game was scarce ; we got a couple of ostriches and a skunk,—or a couple of skunks and an ostrich, I forget which, and it makes less difference to the reader than at the time it did to me. We cooked and lunched on the ground, and turned our faces home-ward with the scanty remainder. The women were busy erecting the wigwams. The ground was frozen, and a large iron bolt, doubtless from some wreck, served as a crowbar to dig holes for the stakes. The encampment was on a hill-side, near a low swamp, which furnished abundance of water, such as it was.

We had scarcely settled down, and I was dreading the stagnant monotony of camp life, when dulness was dis-pelled in a most unwelcome manner. Knots of Indians could be seen in murmuring conversation, whose glances betrayed the bent of their passions. They were again getting impatient of my life, and caresses and flattery were of no avail to stem the rising tide. On the even-ing of the third day, I was summoned out of the lodge by the chief, and followed him in silence, with a trem-bling presentiment of evil. He led me to a spot where twenty or thirty leading spirits in the tribe sat ranged in a circle,—the fatal ring was once more set to insnare me! Once I had escaped. Was it possible to effect a second escape? Everything said no. The chances seemed a hundred to one against it. What had I left unsaid, to tempt their cupidity, to excite alarm, to make them value my safety or dread the effects of harming me? I could think of nothing, and the dismal prospect be-numbed every faculty of my soul. But, as I entered the ominous circle, an access of fresh strength, the courage of desperation, enabled me to bear up with energy against perplexity and fear; to resolve that I would meet them with a steadfast eye and an inflexible mind,—a force which, though springing out of weakness, should prove stronger than their utmost malice.

Having seated myself near the chief, the consultation began and proceeded much as before, but with increased vehemence. Their demonstrations were alarming, but, to my joy, the chief took the same view as in the former council. Would he be able to restrain their savage tempers? His power was great, but there was a limit to its effect, and I feared. In my turn I sought to enforce his views, by arraying all the motives invention could produce, and was able to perceive that they had some weight. Again the matter was canvassed around the ring. There was a hesitation, as if they felt suspicious and unsatisfied. Then they began to cross-examine me; my promises were not explicit enough. What did I mean to give them? The answer did not content them; they wanted more. More or less made no difference to me, and I gave them assurance of all the good things they craved, when we should arrive at *Holland.* Another talk followed, and brought them to a pretty unanimous conclusion, that they would get the presents first, and *decide my fate afterwards;*—a "squeeze-your-orange-and-throw-it-away" policy, in which these rascals seemed to be remarkable adepts.

. The natives had no idea that I could understand their talk, and I was not at all eager to display my acquisitions. In fact, though unable to speak their jargon, my ear had become pretty well trained to interpret it, while my scraps of half Spanish enabled me, without suspicion, to hear, mark, and digest, much of their conversation. This was, in part, acquired in teaching some of them, the youth especially, to speak English and to count—a pursuit in which I engaged partly for their benefit, and partly for my own. Besides aiding me in learning their language, it tended, so far as it diverted their attention, to keep mischief out of their heads, after the manner in which constant employment maintains order in a ship's crew. It added to my knowledge of their character and ways of thinking, so that, in dangerous emergencies, I was able to detect the first symptoms of evil. More than once it enabled me to elude or to nip in the bud dangerous conspiracies, which, if they had gone further, might have proved fatal to me. Circumspection made self-possession more easy. I will confess—though the narrative may have made confession needless—that I am naturally timid, and inclined to the better part of valour. Yet somehow—God helping me—I early learned to hide my constitutional timidity under a show of fearlessness, even in circumstances of great peril. More than once, when a savage drew his knife at me, have I looked him in the eye and disarmed him by a laugh; perhaps laying hold of the instrument of death, trying its edge and praising its qualities, till its owner was shamed into quiet. One piece of English that tickled the chief was the title of "Old Boy," with which (from a conviction of its appropriateness) I early honoured him, and which he appeared to relish as much as if I had called him "His Majesty."

The council, to my great relief, at length broke up, and I returned to my wretched shelter. The chief pointed to my bed, and bade me lie down. I complied, not to sleep, but to adore the Providence that had twice rescued me as from the very jaws of death, to reflect on the past and to speculate on the future. The excitement of the evening kept me wakeful, and the night wore away and the morning dawned, without sleep for a moment visiting my eyes.

CHAPTER VII.

FROM this point we moved again in a north-westerly direction, finding game more plenty, and among other animals captured a species of fox, the first I had seen in the country. The camping-ground selected was a waste more desolate than had yet greeted my sight, even in Patagonia,—a low marsh, surrounded by sand-hills destitute of even the semblance or vestige of vegetation, past or present. The horses were let loose to solve the problem of existence as they could, while my landladies, with their canine assistants, served up a skunk and two ostrich-legs for supper. I thought myself fortunate at getting so ample a meal, having been on short allowance the preceding day.

Here a new torture was inflicted. There had been abundance of voluble hatred against me, as I had too good reason to know, but it was around and behind me. Now, presuming, doubtless on my ignorance of their language, they came to utter their bloodthirsty thoughts in my presence. At night, before retiring, the women began to talk against me, as usual; which never gave me much uneasiness, female opinion not having much force, I suspected, in affairs of state. Two of them had always appeared to bear me a mortal grudge, for what cause I could not conjecture, unless they thought I took up too much of his highness' time, or exerted too much influence over him. But, on the present occasion, the conference was enlarged by the entrance of two or three visitors, whose only errand seemed to be to give the chief gratuitous advice touching the disposal of my person. Though perfectly comprehending the drift of their remarks, I looked as stupid as possible, and bent myself to caress and flatter the old fellow with more than common servility;—patting his breast, telling him what a big, good heart it contained, calling him my *compadre*, and myself his child, his *piconine*, his *muchacho*. So deep was my abasement! To talk of the goodness of a heart beating with cruelty and black with crime! To call that black, greasy, depraved monster my father, and myself his dutiful and affectionate son! It is humiliating to speak of this;—what, let the reader imagine, must it have been to feel it! The bruised reed was well-nigh broken. The courage that sustained me in sharp trials was frittered away piecemeal by incessant irritation. Hope, that kept me from fainting in the fatal ring, vanished with the occasion that invoked it, and a bitter consuming despair hovered over me. Then came dark and distracting thoughts of home, now more distant than ever, to stab my heart, already faint and bleeding. Again was sleep driven from me, but the night passed, and the blessed light of day stole upon me, as with a benediction from heaven.

I arose and rushed into the open air to warm myself by exercise, and when the fire was lighted comforted myself by its kindly heat, and recovered a measure of buoyancy. But the day was wearily spent, and night brought the merciless gossips once more into the lodge. The two squaws led off with words of the most fiendish hate, urging that I should be summarily despatched, and gloating over anticipated vengeance. Tempestuous thoughts and sleepless hours had weakened me in body and mind. The fall of successive drops of water will madden the stoutest brain, and the drop too much had now lighted on my head. I was frenzied; strong passions, hitherto held in check, overmastered me. I rose, threw my cap violently on the ground, stamped, gnashed my teeth, and cursed without restraint. I shook my fists at them, defied their malice, and raved for several minutes, reckless of consequences. What was life to me? They were killing me by inches. Let them do their worst, no matter how soon. The chief was at first startled at such an explosion, and sat looking fixedly upon me, with a dark and clouded brow. It was fortunate that my rage was too impetuous to be contained within the bounds of my Indian-Spanish vocabulary, but breathed itself in good strong Saxon, so that speech could not betray me. For no sooner had the internal pressure been measurably relieved, than a sudden consciousness of error—fatal error—smote me with a new dread. What had I done? Where were my wits, that I should thus toss away life to gratify impotent anger? If my chance of life was worth little to myself, was it worth nothing to others, that I should so trifle with it? With returning sanity of feeling came also a hint of the way to repair my wrong. Without waiting for any questions or wordy explanations, I looked piteously at the chief, pointed to my head, and assured him it was

disordered. I could not help my actions. I was sorry
to make such an exhibition of myself, but it was all my
poor head; and holding on to the poor head with one
hand, I beat it reproachfully with the other, at the same
time giving vent to some unearthly noises by way of
corroboration. The old fellow looked rather dubiously
at this change of scene, and asked whether it was at
them I shook my fists?—At them? No, no! they did
not understand me. My heart was good, like his, but
it was all my head, my poor naughty *cabeza.* Another
thump on my cranium, and a second edition of the howl,
proved sufficient. The plea of insanity was admitted;
he expressed himself satisfied, and explained the incident to the amazed spectators. I drew a long breath
with a returning sense of security, scarcely crediting the
success of the artifice, and almost doubting whether the
whole scene was not a dream. Real or unreal, it was
over, and things were apparently on their former footing.
Only my feminine foes would not be convinced, and
added this crowning indiscretion to the list of my
offences.

We moved the next day in a northerly direction, and
struck the river Santa Cruz, encamping about an eighth
of a mile from its marshy banks, which, at this point,
were bent in a broad, horse-shoe curve. We were surrounded, except on the river-side, by high abrupt sand-
banks, covered in part by underwood of a stunted
growth. The river was narrow, but deep and rapid.
The Indians said it was the Santa Cruz, and that it led
directly to "Holland;" but their lies about that same
Dutch land had long since destroyed all faith in their
words. That it was the Santa Cruz was probable, for I
knew of no other river in these parts; we had passed
Corey Inlet and the Gallegos. The rest of the story I
could only *try* to credit. I tried to urge them on, but
they were not to be hurried. Some of them grumbled
that I had no intention of giving them anything, but
meant to slip from them the first opportunity. No

wonder they thought so; they certainly had not laid me
under very great obligations of gratitude. What on
earth they wanted of me, unless to fat and eat me, was
past conjecture; and my fare had not been of a nature
to induce corpulence, so that this supposition was not
trustworthy. They *said* they wanted me to help to steal
horses. They were bound for the Rio Negro, where they
meant to steal seven hundred horses, of which number
I was to get two. Certainly, I told them, it would be
just the thing; and that was a most excellent reason
for going to " Holland." They would find me a rare
thief; but, however it might be with them, *I* could not
steal without a good stock of rum and tobacco. Was
I insincere in all this? The reader may smile or may
frown, but it was my purpose, if I failed to escape by
way of " Holland," to humour them to the top of their
bent; to ride, hunt, and even *steal* my way into their
confidence;—any way to ensure present safety, and keep
an eye open for future opportunities.

Three or four days were passed in suspense, which was
at last terminated by taking our line of march down the
river. We halted at noon, at a point where the banks
sloped gently to the water's edge, on either side of the
deep and narrow channel. Active preparations were here
commenced for crossing. Part of the horses were driven
across the river, whilst a portion of the tribe were occupied in building boats to ferry their families and goods
across. Their boats are constructed after a simple
fashion. A quantity of bushes are cut and dragged
down to the margin of the water. They take four tent-
stakes, and lay them so as to enclose an area eight feet
square, lashing them firmly together at the four corners.
Four Indians then raise the stakes from the ground,
while others place the skin covering of the tent over the
frame, allowing it to sag down three or four feet. The
edges of the skin are brought over the stakes, and
fastened on the inside. The bushes, made ready for the
purpose, are placed within, tops downward, round the

entire circumference, and secured to the stakes, till the boat is completely timbered up. The bushes keep the skin distended, and give to the vessel an oval shape, so that, though square at the top, it bears a striking re-semblance to a large iron pot. Its length and its breadth of beam are of course equal. When completed, it is firmly lashed from stem to sternpost, and from side to side, with a lariat, or green hide rope, forty feet long, to keep it from spreading or racking. I had no hand in modelling this witch of the wave, but, like an apprentice, did as I was ordered in forwarding the structure, and, when nothing else was required, ".held on to the slack." It was at last completed, like the temple of Solomon, without the sound of axe or hammer; neither bolts, trenails, nor caulking-iron, were required. We carried the barge down, and launched her in the stream. Two paddles were made by lashing two bladebones of the guanaco to sticks. Squaws, pappooses, and baggage, were stowed away, till the boat was laden to the water's edge. I was directed to take passage with the family and household effects of the chief, and seated myself in the centre of the closely-packed craft. One end of a lariat was fastened to the boat, and the other tied to the tail of a horse. A savage mounted, with one rein attached to the wooden bit on the up-stream side. Two others took the oars, one on each side, and a squaw was stationed on the top-gallant forecastle for the purpose of singing, to ensure good luck. All is ready. The old horse wades till the depth of water compels him to swim, and the boat is pushed off The rider floats on the horse's back, kicking the water with his feet, holding the rein in one hand, and grasping the mane with the other. "Chew! chew!" he shouts, at the top of his voice. The black swan in the forecastle opens her capacious mouth and sings, "Yek yah, youri miti! yek yah, youri miti!" The two oarsmen dig away with might and main, while the younger fry swell the chorus with a "Yah! yah! yah!" The boat brings some heavy

lurches to the windward, then yaws off to leeward; all
owing to those lubberly oarsmen not meeting her with
the helm in season. At length, after innumerable
shiftings, we reached the opposite shore, and waded up
on dry land.

Several boats were constructed after the same unique
model, and succeeded in crossing safely. Some of the
horses, being better adapted to towing, were swam back
to repeat the process, and our craft returned for a second
freight. I watched the proceedings from the bank with
intense interest, speculating on the probable consequences of an accident to any of the fleet. Such was
their superstition, that, in the event of any ill befalling
them, they would be quite likely to ascribe it to me,
and serve me worse than Jonah was treated by his shipmates. The swiftness of the current, and the rudeness
of their navigation, made them so liable to mischief,
that it seemed wise to prepare for it; and I at once
began ingratiating myself with two of the worst fellows
in the whole tribe, by professions of special goodwill
and admiration for them, and confidential hints that they
would share more liberally in the bounties of " Holland"
than any of their fellows. Whilst thus engaged, with
cautious glances across the river, to make sure that all
was right, I perceived that there was quite a commotion
among the people below; some were springing upon
their horses—others, ready mounted, were dashing
furiously down the bank. On looking some distance
below, a boat appeared to be in distress; the lariat that
bound it together had snapped asunder, and the pressure within, and the strain of the horse without, had
broken the front stake; the horse, relieved of his freight,
pulled for the shore, and could neither be coaxed nor
beaten into a return to duty. The horsemen on the
banks dashed into the stream, and swam for the wreck,
which contained, among other passengers, a young child.
It was already filled with water, and was partially
turned on her side. The surface of the river was dotted

with dark forms, struggling with the mad current; one horseman after another each grasped a floating object, and made for the shore. The craft had drifted nearly half a mile, and nothing could be made out very distinctly. The squaws, on first perceiving the mischance, watched the wreck, and sung in a loud and plaintive strain, all the while casting unfriendly glances at me, and gradually approaching the place where I stood. My apprehensions were so far confirmed by this movement, that I told John (the name I gave one of my present particular friends), as he loved rum and tobacco, and expected to get any, not to leave me. John saw at a glance what was in the wind, and appreciated both the immediate danger and the ultimate reward of averting it; namely, the privilege of being gloriously drunk at my expense. He told me to go into his hut, and pointed me to the farthest corner; where, I being duly ensconced, he took his station, cutlass in hand, directly in front of me. The singing grew louder, and the voices more numerous about the door; the song was their regular powwow strain, which invariably preluded the killing of a horse. The Indians began to enter the lodge, and looked unutterable things in the direction where I was crouching; the wigwam was soon filled with them, and they were beginning to crowd towards me, when old John opened upon them, and told them they ought to be ashamed of themselves, to come in there in that manner; they did not know what had happened— they did not know whether any lives were lost. They were threatening on account of the death of a child, when, for aught they knew, the child was alive; they had better wait patiently, till they knew more about the matter, before they made any further uproar about it. In this strain he parleyed with them for some time, till they concluded to retire, uttering, as they went, the most horrible sounds. I felt less relief from their absence than if John had not, by implication, fully assented that if the brat was drowned, my life should answer for it.

News soon came that the children were all safe, but that the boat was lost.

An instant change ensued : the fire appeared to be quenched, but I feared it might break out at any moment afresh. Knowing their treachery, I kept a pretty suspicious watch on their movements ; the chief soon came over the river, hurried, perhaps, in his movements by the accident, which he had witnessed from the opposite shore. After conferring with John, and giving him some instructions, and seeing that all was right, he re-embarked for the other shore, as he made it his special business to see that all were passed across in safety. The ferrying ceased as night came on ; the chief was likely to be on the opposite side all night, as there was a good day's work yet to be done before the whole would be transported. I had overheard him giving special orders to keep a good look-out on me during the night. I felt, however, some uneasiness in his absence ; he had been my most powerful protector, having twice, at least, saved me from imminent death.

I now began to revolve in my mind the possibility of escape ; the thought suggested itself that I might steal one of their boats, and drift down the stream. I was long since heartily tired of captivity ; my situation, especially if I was to be held a hostage of Providence for the safe ferriage of the tribe, was desperate. But on second thought, I did not know that this was certainly the Santa Cruz ; if it was, I was furthermore ignorant of our distance from the sea. I knew of no white settlement on or near the river ; none, I remembered, was laid down in the chart ; if such a settlement existed, I might hope to reach it in a *boat*, but a voyage in such a craft as one of these would be as hazardous as that of the wise men of Gotham. If there was no such settlement, and "Holland" was Patagonian for Utopia, my only chance, short of drifting in my leathern sack out to sea, would be to land on some island, in case an island there were ; and then what should I live on after landing? Berries I had never seen, except once or twice. Besides, my stolen craft could not be *paddled*— the Indians had too good ears for that; I must follow the channel passively, through all its course, which was terribly crooked, while its rapidity increased the risk that the ungainly vehicle would be disabled. On the whole, it was so doubtful whether I could reach any particular place, or escape starvation after I got there, and so certain that failure would be death, the project seemed a forlorn hope. But then, again, it was not more forlorn than my present situation., So my poor mind vibrated between dangers—the danger of remaining where I was—the danger that I should escape only from the frying-pan into the fire. At last, as I *felt* the frying-pan, and only *feared* the fire, I concluded to try.

Crawling as noiselessly as possible from my resting-place, I stole softly out, and made for the river. Alack! in calculating the chances, I had not once thought of four-footed enemies, and they were upon me before I was halfway to the shore,—a half-dozen dogs, barking loud enough to wake the whole encampment. I retreated incontinently to the lodge, and succeeded in getting quietly into my quarters again, not without some inward spasms. It was all for the best, no doubt, but it was not just then easy to think so, or *possible* to *feel* so; and therefore, after a little time, I once more emerged from the lodge, and stole towards the river by a different track, hoping to elude those infernal dogs; but they, or some others, were on the alert, and came pell-mell upon my rear, barking more uproariously than before. I cursed the dogs, their masters, and my own folly, and gave up the attempt.

The ferrying recommenced the next morning; and before night the whole tribe were safely landed, with their effects, on the west side of the river, and their wigwams were all pitched. We were short of provisions; but this was a common case, and I was accustomed to it. I got an occasional morsel of grease, sufficient to keep starvation at bay; but illness, with bad and insufficient food, had greatly emaciated me, till I was a spectacle but few degrees above the living skeleton. But hope was still in the ascendant, and I had no idea of lying down to die till I was quite sure my time had come. We continued our wanderings the next day in a westerly direction, slaying every living creature that came within reach, from a skunk to a guanaco. This was a great disappointment, as I hoped we should go down the river, the direction in which they said "Holland" lay, and the only direction in which we were likely to strike a white settlement, if any existed on the Atlantic coast. But my remonstrances on this head were vain; they would go where they pleased, and I must go with them. Time dragged heavily; hours seemed days, and days weeks. But impatience is no virtue, and submission was imperative.

The country hereabout was more broken and mountainous than any we had before traversed, with a more abundant growth of bushes, and some clumps of stunted trees here and there. As we proceeded, keeping still to the north-west, game was more plenty. We came to two ponds, or small lakes, one of not more than four acres in extent, the other considerably larger. The latter was shallow, at least near the shore, as some ostriches pursued by the Indians ran into it, and their pursuers waded after, and succeeded in capturing them.

At one time I observed a large scar in the calf of the chief's leg—the mark of a wound that must have been inflicted a long time before, as it was completely healed. Its depression was so great as to indicate a very severe cut, unless the old fellow had grown uncommonly fat since he received it. On inquiring the cause of it, he said it was from a wound inflicted by the Alanagros, a tribe inhabiting a country to the northward. The name he gave them signifies the blacks; and, from the manner in which he spoke of them, I inferred they were in some respects superior to the Patagonians. He said v were armed with cutlasses and very long knives,.

had tobacco, and plenty of horses; and I conjectured that they might have been a party of Spanish Americans, or one of the mixed races of Spanish origin. The fight, he said, arose on occasion of his tribe being on a horse-stealing expedition; they encamped a short distance off, and at night he made a descent on the Alanagros, killed some of them, and plundered their camp, carrying off many of their horses. The plundered tribe rallied, hotly pursued them, and recaptured a part of the booty; in the struggle wounding him with a cutlass, and, as I judged by appearances, cutting to the bone. He told the story with great spirit, slashing right and left, and grunting with extraordinary emphasis, as if to give an impression that good hard blows were given and taken; but I afterwards learned that it was a cowardly running fight, in which more sweat than blood was spilled.

Nothing of importance occurred at our encampment near the lakes, except—what was a very noteworthy fact with me—such an abundance of ostrich that I was surfeited with the delicious fare, and was compelled by the chief to take a horse-rein emetic,—a more precise description of which the reader will have no difficulty in excusing. Had I not so completely disavowed the medical character, the chief might probably have allowed me to feel my own pulse—if I could find it—and to prescribe for myself; but the renunciation of professional honours brought me under the sanitary, as well as the political jurisdiction of Parosilver.

Our line of march was now in a northerly direction, soon deflecting to the eastward,—a movement that revived my sinking hopes. There seemed to be some prospect of striking the Atlantic coast, and coming within reach of civilized men. On our way we observed the tracks of some animals different from any I had met with. The chief said it was the *limerer*, with which lucid definition I was fain to be content; and, as no specimens were visible, the inquisitive naturalist must trust to his imagination for the rest.

CHAPTER VIII.

My hopes were soon cast down, by a decided movement to the westward. Every step, I was convinced, lengthened the distance between me and the spot where my most earnest wishes centred; for, though I knew not of any settlement in this barren region, yet it was pretty certain that if there was one it must be sought in the line of the Santa Cruz. Of our latitude and longitude I could form no decisive judgment; but by the aid of the sun, of which occasional glimpses were caught, it was easy to take note of our direction, and I never retired to rest without taking landmarks, and satisfying myself as nearly as possible as to our whereabouts. At night there was a renewal of the discussions which had once so nearly turned my brain, and now at times came near verifying the plea which then saved me from destruction; but I was enabled to keep my feelings in more equal check. Disappointed and care-worn, I spent the night in commending myself to the mercy and good providence of God, praying that he would soften the heart of the savage and open a way of deliverance.

Among other matters that excited my curiosity, I was anxious to know whether the Indians were expert swimmers. The only occasion on which I had seen them atttempt it was at the time of the accident in crossing the river. Then two of them swam across, while the others floated on their horses' backs, clinging to the mane. In answer to some questions dropped on the subject, the chief assured me that they were all expert swimmers, and could stretch off a long distance without resting, as they would show me, but that the coldness of the season made the experiment too unpleasant. Others of the tribe told the same story. The question was interesting for obvious reasons. I had thought a time might come when it would be a very practical one.

Some new specimens of birds made their appearance from time to time. One was a large black bird, resembling the turkey-buzzard, and subsisting on carrion. Another resembled the snow-birds of the north. I had also seen, near the sea-shore and by the lakes, several species of water-fowl,—one not unlike the wild-goose, but the chief said they were not good for food.

Our course, the next day, was northward, and the day following turned once more decidedly towards the east, whereat my hopes, varying with the compass, began to revive, though their buoyancy was tempered by experience of the uncertainty of Indian movements. Observing a spot covered with small trees, over which a great number of carrion birds hovered, we approached and found the carcass of a poor old guanaco, which had most likely paid the debt of nature without compulsion, and was stripped of its flesh by the birds. The chief broke some of the bones and eagerly sucked the marrow, and then picked up the remainder to add to the domestic stock of grease.

At the close of the next day we brought up at a ravine, and found our camp by following it a short distance to a low flat. Proceeding to the eastward all the next day, we ascended a high eminence, from which the chief pointed in a south-westerly direction, and said that "Holland" lay *there*. I strained my eyes in the quarter indicated, without, however, making any discoveries, and with a strong disposition to think the Old Boy was hoaxing me. At dark we defiled down a steep declivity, and pitched our tents on the border of an extensive marsh covered with ice. Here I renewed my arguments for speeding our way to the promised land, dilating on the qualities of the promised rum in a style that would have astonished the advocates of the Maine liquor law, and impaired the confidence of those who had reasonably regarded me as a strict temperance man. Indeed, the antics and grimace with which I enforced the description, and illustrated the jovial effects of the creature,—the

boasts of how I would teach them, by its aid, to throw
the lasso, and perform most astonishing feats of horse-
stealing and riding,—might have induced a suspicion
that I knew more of it than mere observation or fancy
could teach.   But, however it may affect my reader, it
produced unmistakable contentment and satisfaction to
my Patagonian auditors; and that was what I aimed at.
They looked and listened with watering mouths and
hoarse laughter, giving token that the balmy description
was appreciated to a most desirable degree.   So evident
was the impression that I spent the next day running
about and giving line upon line to the most influential
of the tribe, and succeeded as I thought, in awakening
a degree of enthusiasm to move towards the place where
all these good things were to be got.   In confirmation
of this, I had the satisfaction of being called at night to
attend a solemn council.

It was a peaceful gathering,—they left their weapons
behind,—but it contemplated only a sort of prelimi-
nary inquiry; the Patagonians know how to make their
forms of procedure as tedious as any of our courts of
law, summary as are many of their dealings.   They
examined and cross-examined very strictly, sifting my
story with a severity which showed that they were in
earnest, and at the same time a little suspicious.   It
was necessary to be on my guard at all points; and
if they had been more docile learners of arithmetic,
and able to stick on questions of number and quantity,
it might have been a harder matter to satisfy them.
But, on the whole, the old story was stuck to with a
degree of consistency that produced the desired effect.
Their confidence was perceptibly raised, and after a
good deal of talk, the council adjourned, every one more
than ever disposed to visit "Holland."

While at this encampment I observed on the ground
about a dozen large oyster-shells, that appeared to have
been recently opened.   These were the first and only
shells of the kind I saw in the country.   I inquired if they

were plenty in that vicinity. They said they were not; none of the tribe seemed to know where they came from, or anything about them. The chief said that he and his people did not relish oysters, but other Indians ate them. He did not like fish of any kind; no fish had grease enough for them; none of *his* Indians ate fish. This, and some similar incidents and conversations, convinced me that there were other Indian tribes in the vicinity. On one occasion I had noticed some places where a tribe, probably as numerous as our own, had encamped. Their fires appeared to have been very recently extinguished. Our tribe appeared to be considerably disturbed at these discoveries, and I judged that they were the traces of some enemies. It is certain that my captors had seen some desperate fights, of which they bore the marks on their persons. One of them had a deep scar on his breast, which he said was the mark of an arrow-shot received from the "*Yamaschoner*" Indians, a tribe that use the bow and arrow. His description suggested the probability that these were the Terra-del-Fuego Indians; but, on mentioning the conjecture at a later period to a person I met at the Chilian penal settlement, he informed me that those islanders invariably shoot *poisoned* arrows, which would not leave the victim much leisure to describe their effect. The scar in question was a deep one, in the region of the heart; and while I was examining it, the chief remarked that the arrow passed through his body and came out at his back. On examination, a distinct scar was visible on his back, so far corresponding in form and direction with the one in front, that it seemed likely to have been made by the same weapon. But how the arrow could have transfixed him through the chest, without wounding the vital organs, was not easily to be conjectured. The only explanation I could conceive of was, that the fellow's heart was so much harder than any material used for arrow heads, that the missile, instead of penetrating that important organ, had

glanced aside and passed without mortal hurt. Enough
had been developed to assure me that the tribe generally
had hearts of no ordinary toughness, capable of serving
them for all practical purposes wherein impenetrable
stuff was in request; but the tale of this miraculous
escape gave a new impression of obduracy, and entitled
the hero to bear the palm among his fellows. I pre-
tended to pity him for his former sufferings, and went
so far as to volunteer—in case I should ever be permitted to enter the enemy's territory—to make mince-
meat of some of them, and so to avenge his cruel
injuries. This spontaneous sympathy and forwardness
to take up his quarrel was exceedingly gratifying to the
sufferer and to the chief, and drew from them a more
particular narrative of the combat.

They were out on a horse-stealing expedition,—the
usual occasion, it seems, of Patagonian fights,—and
made a swoop upon the camp of another tribe. The
objects of this felonious invasion asserted title to the
horses in their possession by certain tangible arguments,
and induced a mortal combat. And now Old Boy
waxed eloquent, and especially displayed that prime
ingredient, "action." His broad-sword exercise was
really animated, and taught us "how fields were won,"
or would have done so, but that, while his right hand
was slashing the air with his good steel, his left would
hold the bridle-rein, and his heels involuntarily drive the
spur;—in short, though it was a part on which he did not
linger in the narration any more than in the act, there
was some tall running on the occasion. So artlessly was
the tale told, that while the hero was cutting and thrust-
ing and grunting, to make due impression of the
desperate bravery displayed in the encounter, his
subordinate action clearly depicted a running and
retreating fight, and convinced me that they got a sound
drubbing for their pains. He said he killed one Indian,
with an air that would have done justice to the slaying
of a regiment. Shocking to relate, there were found

persons who slanderously reported to me that Old Boy's legs had the unhappy propensity of Pat O'Flaherty's, whose heart was as brave as any man's, but his cowardly legs ran away with his body; and they scrupled not to affirm that in this same hard-fought battle he crawled into the bushes, and there secreted himself till the cessation of hostilities enabled him to rejoin his tribe.

The reader has doubtless noticed that "the tribe" has been all along anonymous. The explanation comes rather late, but, in point of fact, I never could learn that they had any distinctive name; they never used any. Indeed proper names are very seldom heard. Even in conversation concerning each other, they managed to avoid "naming names" as strictly as so many honourable senators, though for no reason that I could discover. By signs and gestures, and other hints, they indicated the personal subject of remark, and seemed to suffer no inconvenience from what would be felt among us as a serious want.

While out hunting one day with the chief, we ascended a slight eminence, commanding a view of an extensive plain. The chief suddenly stopped his horse, and looked steadily forward. I bent my eyes in the same direction, and saw two or three mounted Indians moving towards a common point. There was nothing unusual to be seen, but Old Boy seemed to discover something. I inquired what it was. He answered by pointing; and, on a second view, I observed a horse loose, which I took to be that of some Indian temporarily dismounted. But the chief said they were about to catch a wild horse, and forthwith dashed off at a furious rate, bidding me follow. We were rapidly nearing the spot, when the two in advance of us put their horses at top speed towards the lone horse that was standing beside a clump of bushes. It suddenly ran before its pursuers, followed by two colts from the thicket. The colts appeared to be one or two years old, and were doubtless following their dam. One Indian singled out the mare, and another the larger

colt. The little one did not lag behind. The chief and
myself followed at a pace which would have made a
single misstep fatal to our necks; but fortunately our
horses proved sure-footed. On we dashed, helter-skelter,
in a direction to head off the pursuers, and to place ourselves nearest to the affrighted animals. The mare yet
holds the lead, and fairly tears up the soil with her
flashing hoofs. An Indian, in close pursuit, presently ·
swings his lariat about his head; but she makes a curve
in her course, and springs beyond the reach of his aim.
Her pursuer once more gains on her; again the lariat
swings through the air,—he lets go,—the noose catches
her neck,—the hunter's horse turns suddenly off, and the
rope, securely attached to the saddle, brings the poor
captive headlong to the ground. The trained horse
keeps a strain on the noose sufficient to prevent her
from rising, while the hunter dismounts and secures his
prize. The colts shared the same fate, and, with the
mother, were subdued and made useful to the tribe.

The scenes and reminiscences I have described did not
prevent the matter of most absorbing interest to myself—
the projected visit to "Holland"—from engaging due attention. The chief came home from the council full of it.
He was in royal goodhumour, and talked about it half
the night; but several objections arose, which it was
necessary for me to dispose of. These were met, apparently, to his full satisfaction. One of the most serious
was the fear that the white men would revenge upon
him the murder of Captain Eaton. I assured him that
so long as I was with him he had nothing to fear on
that score; the people were all mine, and would do, or
refrain from doing, whatever I should bid them. They
would not dare to lift their hands against him contrary
to my orders, or refuse to deliver what articles I chose
to demand. Nothing, I found, would do, but the asser-
tion of absolute supremacy over all white men whatever,
the world around; less than this would not secure the
confidence of these savages, and I regulated my speech

by the necessities of the case. The chief inquired, a dozen times over, what I would say to the white men, and I as often rehearsed an address for the occasion. At last his curiosity seemed abated, and we fell asleep.

Early the next morning we were up and stirring, and the chief having adjusted his toilet with care, a slight breakfast was made ready. This over, his highness stood forth, and from the door of his lodge made an official address to the tribe, wherein he set out the advantages of a visit to "Holland," and suggested the most expedient style of making it. He advised that a few only of the tribe should be deputed, with himself, to accompany me, and receive the stores of rum, tobacco, bread, rice, tea, butter, beads, brass, copper, and so forth, that were to be forthcoming, as the expression of my gratitude for the distinguished consideration with which they had treated me. Though royal speeches seldom excite any jealousy of plagiarism, and it may seem a little captious on my part to make such a charge, it is due to "the truth of history" to declare, that herein the great Parosilver did but repeat a suggestion which he did me the honour to receive with favour over-night. It was not deemed essential to the case to inform his highness of *all* the reasons that led me to wish for as small an escort as the nature of the business would admit of. On the contrary, acting upon the profound maxim, that one *sufficient* reason is as good as a dozen, and better than that number of questionable ones, I merely advised, that, after the experience which Captain Eaton and others had had of Patagonian prowess, the sight of too many of his giants would frighten away the whites, and prevent all beneficial communication with them; while the presence of a small deputation would be a pledge of their pacific inclinations. The speech from the throne proved less *moving* than most of the chief's effusions; his lieges listened with great interest, and an earnest debate sprung up, at the conclusion of which it was decided that the chief, with four other

Indians and their squaws, should be my body-guard, the rest of the tribe to follow after. Another old woman begged to go with us, which was agreed to. The horse I had been in the habit of riding was lame, and unfit for service; another was procured for me.

Our simple preparations for departure were soon made, and as we were about to start they all began bringing their dirty children to me, and requesting that I would bring brass and beads for them all; which was gravely promised, much to their satisfaction. There remained the last act in the comedy for which I had been long rehearsing,—if, indeed, it did not turn out a tragedy. The idea had early occurred to me, that if I had some object to which I appeared very much attached, it might prove to be for my advantage; the Indians might hold it, in my absence at any time, as a sort of surety for my return. A belle from among the beauties of the tribe would be effectual to that end; but, if no sentiments of virtue had restrained me from this expedient, the filth and unsightliness of them all were enough to ensure continence. I chose, therefore, a little white dog for a pet,—a dirty, thievish little rascal;—but I fondled him in the style proper to a violent attachment. It is true that when I saw him licking the meat designed for our repast it was not easy to refrain from kicking his worthless brains out; but this was a trifle to other things I had to endure, and I made myself apparently so fond of him that the reality of the case was never suspected. Now and then I indemnified myself by giving him, when unobserved, a smart rapping for his misdeeds, though such chastisement made but a slight impression on the object of it. As we were about setting out, I was asked if I intended to take my dog. No, I told them, he would be better off there, and when I returned he should have some bread and other dainties to eat. The ruse more than answered its expected end, in lulling all suspicion of my sincerity.

At last we were under way. The grand crisis to which

all my diplomacy and the utmost licence of fiction had tended was near at hand. A strong hope of deliverance braced my spirits, shaded, it is true, by a natural apprehension of possible failure, and of the consequences that might follow. With no great elation of spirits, but with a stern, severe tension of all my mental energies, and a concentration of them into one focus of resolve, I waved a farewell, which I hoped might be everlasting, to the accursed gang of robbers who had tormented me so many tedious weeks. "Good-by to Patagonia!" I mentally ejaculated, and struck off with my escort; but had not gone more than an eighth of a mile, when the party wheeled about and ordered me to follow them back to the camp! I remonstrated, but it was of no use, and with a heavy heart I found myself once more in my dirty corner of a wigwam. The horses were turned adrift without a word of explanation, and the Indians sat down to a game of cards, with as much indifference to everything else as if the events of the past forty-eight hours had been a feverish dream. What could be the meaning of it? I questioned the chief. He merely replied that he would go by and by,—by and by; which, being interpreted, probably meant when he pleased, and that convenient season might never arrive! After I had teased him for a long time he took me to the door of the lodge, and, pointing to the river, said it was "no good then;" it would be "good" at night. What the state of the river, which was a shallow stream, a branch of the Santa Cruz, had to do with the matter, I could not divine, and was half inclined to vote myself fairly outwitted by the Old Boy.

The day, along one, at last wore away, and at night we once more set off. We crossed the frozen marsh, and forded the river, and, after going about two miles, stopped for repose. We took no camp equipage, and had to shelter ourselves for the night under the lee of a clump of bushes. We thrust our feet into the thicket, while our heads lodged out of doors. In this interesting

attitude I was made to repeat my wearisome detail of
promises, and to rehearse once more my contemplated
speech to the white men; which done, we dropped
asleep. Waking early the next morning, I found my
head and shoulders covered with a fleecy mantle of
snow. Would the fortune of my expedition fall as
lightly on me? I shook it off, turned up my coat-
collar, pulled my poor, more than half worn-out cap
over my ears, and so, partially protected from the storm,
rolled over, and again sunk into a slumber. The storm
ceased at dawn of day. I rose and went in search of
fuel, while my dark companions still slept profoundly.
In an hour or two they roused themselves, and kindled
a fire. Meat, from a store brought along for our provision on the way, was cooked, and served for breakfast.
The scanty meal being despatched, our horses were
driven in, lassoed, mounted, and we resumed our journey, in a south-easterly direction. At the end of about
three miles another halt was called, a fire was built to
warm by, and the horses were watered. The order of
arrangements was discussed, and a fresh edition of the
promises and the speech critically listened to. Changing
our course a little to the right, we soon struck the Santa
Cruz. The Indians pointed far down the stream, and
said, "There is Holland." I strained my eyes in the
direction pointed out, and thought I could discern an
island with several small huts upon it. A mile or two
further on the north bank brought us to the mouth of
the river, in prospect of the Atlantic. The island was
directly opposite the mouth, and the lower part only appeared to be inhabited. We halted. The Indians
pointed towards it, exclaiming, "Esta Holland sarvey!
muchas casas, mucho mucho hombres, teme mucho
aquadiente, mucho travac, yeruen, arenar, arose!"—This
is Holland, and has plenty of houses, and abundance of
men,—plenty of rum, tobacco, bread, tea, flour, and
rice! I surveyed the spot in silence. This island was
of considerable extent, lying two-thirds across the wide

mouth of the river, its surface dotted over with little knolls or hillocks of earth. Could it be that these were dwellings inhabited by white men?

Our horses' heads were now turned from the shore, and we rode back about an eighth of a mile to a large clump of bushes, unsaddled our beasts, and waited some time for the rest of our company, who had fallen in the rear. They came at last, our horses were turned adrift, fire was lighted, and, as the day was far spent, supper was in order. Then ensued a repetition—a final one, I trusted—of the grand present to be levied on the Hollanders, and of the speech which was to draw them out. The Indians arranged that I was to hoist the English flag,—the colours of the unfortunate brig Avon, which they had brought along at my request,—and then to walk the shore to attract the attention of the islanders. On the approach of a boat, I was to be kept back from the beach, to prevent escape; for I found that they were not, after all, as well assured of my good faith as might have been desirable. They thought, moreover, that when the white men saw a prisoner with them, they would come ashore to parley, and offer presents to effect his release; in that case, there might be a chance, if the negotiation proved unsatisfactory, to take bonds of fate in the form of another captive or two. So, at least there was ground to suspect,—and some cause to fear that the rascals might prove too shrewd for all of us!

After talking till a late hour, the Indians threw themselves upon the ground, stuck their feet into the bushes, and were soon fast asleep. I consulted the chief as to the propriety of modifying this arrangement, by placing our heads, rather than our feet, under cover, since both could not be accommodated. He declined any innovations, and told me to go to sleep. I stretched myself on the ground, but as to sleep, that was out of the question. I lay all night, thinking over all possible expedients for escape. We had no materials for a boat or raft of any description, and it was impossible to

think of any plan that promised success; so that, after
tossing, in body and mind, through the weary hours of
night, I could only resolve to wait the course of events,
and to take advantage of the first opportunity affording
a reasonable hope of deliverance from this horrid captivity. Snow, sleet, and rain, fell during the night; and
I rose early, thoroughly chilled, every tooth chattering.
A fire was kindled, and the last morsel of meat that
remained to us was cooked and eaten. The weather
continued squally till the middle of the afternoon.

After breakfast the chief went with me to the shore,
bearing the flag. On the beach I found a strip of thick
board, to which I fastened the colours, and then planted
it in the sand. The bushes around, which have a kind
of oily leaf and readily ignite, were set on fire. I then
walked the beach,—but no boat came. When it cleared
up sufficiently to see, I observed little objects moving
about on the island. The day wore away with fruitless
attempts to attract their attention. With an aching
heart I returned, at dark, to the camping-ground. On
this island my hopes had so long centred,—if they were
now to be disappointed, how could I endure it? The
Indians began to talk of rejoining the tribe the following day. I opposed the motion with all the dissuasives
at command, assuring them that, at sight of our flag,
the islanders would surely come over in a boat, and
that, if they would only wait a little, they could go over
to the island and enjoy themselves to their hearts' content; representing the absolute necessity that I should
procure the rum, &c., we had talked off, and how em-
barrassing it would be to go back to the tribe empty
handed, after all that had been said, to be ridiculed and
reproached. It would never do. Our conversation was
continued till quite late, when we ranged ourselves,
hungry and weary, for another night. For hours I was
unable to sleep. The uncertainties of my situation
oppressed me, and I lay restless, with anxiety inex-
pressible, inconceivable by those whom Providence has
preserved from similar straits. It was a season of deep,

suppressed, silent misery, in which the heart found no
relief but in mute supplication to Him who was alone
able to deliver. Towards morning, exhausted with the
intensity of emotion acting on an enfeebled body, I
slept a little, and woke at early dawn, to a fresh consciousness of my critical position.

The weather had been fair during the night, but
there were now indications of another snow-storm. I
waited long and impatiently for my companions to
awake, and at last started off in quest of fuel; on returning with which they bestirred themselves and
started a fire, which warmed our half-benumbed limbs.
There lay the little island, beautiful to eyes that longed,
like mine, for a habitation of sympathizing men, about
a mile and a half distant; it almost seemed to recede
while I gazed, so low had my hopes sunken, under the
pressure of disappointment and bitter uncertainty. A
violent snow-storm soon setting in, it was hidden from
view; everything seemed to be against me. It
slackened and partially cleared up: then came another
gust, filling the air and shutting up the prospect. In
this way it continued till past noon; at intervals, as
the sky lighted up, I took a firebrand, and set fire to
the bushes on the beach, and then hoisted the flag again,
walking wearily to and fro, till the storm ceased and
the sky became clear. The chief concealed himself in a
clump of bushes, and sat watching, with cat-like vigilance, the movements of the islanders. After some
time, he said a boat was coming; I scarcely durst look
in the direction indicated, lest I should experience a
fresh disappointment; but I did look, and saw, to my
great joy, a boat launched, with four or five men on
board, and pushing off the shore. On they came; the
chief reported his discovery, and the rest of the Indians
came to the beach, where I was still walking backward
and forward. The boat approached, not directly off
where I was, but an eighth of a mile, perhaps, to the
windward, and there lay on her oars.

The Indians hereupon ordered me to return to the

camping-ground; but, without heeding them, I set off
at a full run towards the boat. They hotly pursued, I
occasionally turning and telling them to come on—I
only wanted to see the boat. "Stop! Stop!" they
bawled. "Now, my legs," said I, "if ever you want
to serve me, this is the time." I had one advantage
over my pursuers; my shoes, though much the worse
for wear, protected my feet from the sharp stones,
which cut theirs at every step; but, under all disadvan-
tages, I found they made about equal speed with myself.
As I gained a point opposite the boat, the Indians
slackened their speed, and looked uneasily at me; the
man in the stern of the boat hailed me, inquiring what
Indians these were, what number of them, and how I
came among them. I replied in as few words as possible, and told him we wished to cross to the island.
He shook his head; they were bad fellows, he said; he
could not take me with the Indians. They began to
pull away! I made signs of distress, and waved them
to return, shouting to them through my hands. The
boat was again backed within hailing distance. "Will
you look out for me if I come by myself?" "Yes!"
was the prompt reply. The Indians all this time had
kept within ten or fifteen feet of me, with their hands
on their knives, and reiterating their commands to
come back, at the same time edging towards me in a
threatening manner. "Yes, yes," I told them, "in a
moment," but I wanted to look at the boat,—taking
care, however, to make good my distance from them.
At the instant of hearing the welcome assurance that I
should be cared for, I drew out the watch (which I had
brought, according to promise, to have a new crystal
inserted at Holland), and threw it into the bushes; the
salt water would spoil it, and, if I *should* be retaken,
the spoiling of that would be an aggravation which
might prove fatal. At the same moment I gave a
plunge headlong into the river; my clothes and shoes
encumbered me, and the surf, agitated by a high wind,

THE ESCAPE.

rolled in heavy seas upon the shore. The boat was forty or fifty yards off; and, as the wind did not blow square in shore, drifted, so as to increase the original distance, unless counteracted by the crew. Whether the boat was backed up towards me, I could not determine; my head was a great part of the time under water, my eyes blinded with the surf, and most strenuous exertion was necessary to live in such a sea. As I approached the boat I could see several guns, pointed, apparently, at me. Perhaps we had misunderstood each other—perhaps they viewed me as an enemy! In fact they were aimed to keep the Indians from following me into the water, which they did not attempt. My strength was fast failing me; the man at the helm, perceiving it, stretched out a rifle at arm's length. The muzzle dropped into the water, and arrested my feeble vision. Summoning all my remaining energy, I grasped it, and was drawn towards the boat; a sense of relief shot through and revived me, but revived also such a dread lest the Indians should give chase, that I begged them to pull away—I could hold on. The man reached down, and seized me by the collar, and ordered his men to ply their oars. They had made but a few strokes, when a simultaneous cry broke from their lips, "Pull the dear man in! Pull the dear man in!" They let fall their oars, laid hold of me, and, in their effort to drag me over the side of their whale-boat, I received some injury. I requested that they would let me help myself; and, working my body up sufficiently to get one knee over the gunwale, I gave a spring, with what strength was left me, and fell into the bottom of the boat. They kindly offered to strip me and put on dry clothes; but I told them, if they would only work the boat further from the shore, I would take care of myself. They pulled away, while I crawled forward, divested myself of my coat, and put on one belonging to one of the crew. Conversation, which was attempted, was impossible; it was one of the coldest days of a Patagonian winter: I was chilled through, and could only articulate, "I ca-n't ta-lk now; I'll ta-lk by a-nd by." Some liquor, bread, and tobacco, which had been put on board for my ransom, on supposition that this was what the signal meant, was produced for my refreshment. The sea was heavy, with a strong head-wind; so that, though the men toiled vigorously, our progress was slow. I was soon comfortably warmed by the stimulants provided, and offered to lend a hand at the oar, but the offer was declined. The shouts and screams of the Indians, which had followed me into the water, and rung hideously in my ears while struggling for life in the surf, were kept up till distance made them inaudible. Whether they found the watch, whose mysterious tick at once awed and delighted them, and restored it to its place of state in the chief's lodge, or whether it still lies rusting in the sands by the sea-shore, is a problem unsolved.

The boat at last grounded on the northern shore of the island; Mr. Hall, the gentleman who commanded the party, supported my tottering frame in landing; and, as we stepped upon the shore, welcomed me to their island. I grasped his hand, and stammered my thanks for this deliverance, and lifted a tearful eye to heaven, in silent gratitude to God. I was then pointed to a cabin near by, where a comfortable fire was ready for me. "Now," I heard Mr. Hall say, "let us fire a salute of welcome to the stranger. Make ready! present! fire!" Off went all their muskets, and a very cordial salute it appeared to be. He soon followed me, took me to his own dwelling, supplied me with dry clothing, and, above all, warmed me in the kindly glow of as generous a heart as ever beat in human bosom.

I was captured by the savages on the 1st of May, and landed upon the island on the 7th of August.

CHAPTER IX.

AFTER getting sufficiently thawed out, I gave a synopsis of my adventures. The cook presently laid the table, and brought in supper. I ate heartily of bread and Irish pork, and drank tea raised in Brazil, called *matte*. It may not compare favourably with the produce of China, but to me it was a delicious beverage. I had been in captivity ninety-seven days, living as the reader has seen. Although I partook freely of supper,—too freely for one in my weak condition,—I rose from the meal with as keen an appetite as I brought to it. I again expressed to Mr. Hall, on learning his name, my gratitude at finding myself, through his timely assistance, among friends, though a stranger. He cordially sympathized with me, observing that he had been a prisoner among the Patagonians for one day only, but had seen enough in that short time to be convinced that a life of ninety-seven days with them must have been dreadful indeed.

After supper the boat was hauled up on the island. Pipes and tobacco were furnished, and I passed in the society of my deliverers one of the happiest evenings of my whole life. The change was so great, from the miserable and almost hopeless existence I had so long lived, that my joy exceeded all bounds. My heart overflowed with gratitude. Words could not then, and cannot now, convey any adequate impression of my feelings,—of the freedom and joy that animated me, on being snatched from perils, privations, and enemies, and placed, as in a moment, in security, in plenty, and in the society of friends. It seemed like a dream, the change was so sudden and so total.

The little house which for the present I called my home, and which, in fact, appeared to me at the time the pleasantest dwelling I had ever seen, was about twelve by fifteen feet upon the ground, built of boards and scantling, and lined with blue Kentucky jean. The fire-place was in the middle of one end, and a door opened at the opposite extremity. Two large closets were parted off, the one used as a cupboard, and the other for stores. Each side was lighted by a window containing four panes of seven-by-nine glass. Two comfortable settees, pro-bably saved from some wreck, lined the sides of the room, and a good-sized hard-wood table occupied the centre. It was floored overhead, and a trap-door opened into a sleeping apartment, fitted with two little berths,—one for Mr. Hall, and the other for Mr. Morrison, the Scotchman.

As we have described the interior of our snug little cottage, we will bestow a word or two on its exterior and surroundings. Its cracks and joints, over the roof and walls, were covered with strips of tarred duck, and battened with narrow pieces of thin board. It was situated on a little mound of guano, perhaps four feet high, and was banked up to the windows with the same material. The height of the walls above the embank-ment was about seven feet, the embankment three feet more. A ship's bell was suspended on the north-east corner of the house, to notify the workmen of the hours of labour and of their meals. Sea Lion Island, as it is called,—the name "Holland" was probably corrupted by the Indians, from the word *island*, indistinctly pro-nounced in their hearing,—is about a mile and a quarter long from north to south, with an average width of an eighth of a mile, and is covered over its entire surface with low evergreen bushes. The settlement was made by an English company, for the purpose of collecting guano and preparing it for exportation, and was situated on the southern extremity.

Our social evening was prolonged to a late hour, the moments sped by the stimulus of novel enjoyment. One of the settees was assigned for my couch, bedclothes were provided, and a bag filled with ships' colours and other articles served for a pillow. Before committing ourselves to repose, however, we discussed the probability of an invasion from the continent, and came to the conclusion that nothing was to be feared in that quarter before morning. Old Boy and his party, it was obvious, would have to return to the main body of the tribe for reinforcements and naval equipage before attempting pursuit, as they had no materials for the construction of boats or rafts, even if they would dare to tempt salt water in their leathern sacks. We accordingly dismissed the subject for the time, and Mr. Hall and the Scotchman, having cared for my comfort with anxious kindness, disappeared through the trap-door, leaving behind a friendly benediction. The little cottage was warm; my couch was the perfection of comfort, in contrast with that which had been my lot for ninety-seven wretched nights. Above all, for the first time in so many weeks, I could lie down without the fear of treachery and violence. I was secure from savages. This indeed was luxury. I slept soundly, vying in the profundity of slumber with the immortal seven, till late in the morning. Daylight at length had dispossessed the darkness of every part of the interior, and I awoke. It was no dream. I was indeed free. Rude but unmistakable evidences of civilization surrounded me. The adventures of the preceding day flashed vividly on my hitherto clouded mind,—the suspense, the struggle, the seasonable rescue, the rejoicing welcome, the spontaneous and subduing kindnesses,—and a warm gush of tender and grateful emotion from my inmost soul thrilled and suffused my whole being. While these emotions were subsiding from the fervour of their first impulse, and the mind was gliding away into a delicious and confused reverie, wherein all manner of delight seemed to encircle me as with an atmosphere, in whose genial glow all past suffering existed only for the heightening of present enjoyment, the trap-door overhead was lifted, and my generous friends dropped down with a hearty salutation.

I sprang from my couch, as good as new, and younger than ever. A cheerful coal-fire was soon burning in the grate, the room was swept, breakfast was brought in and despatched, the bell rang, and the men issued forth to their daily labours, while I went out to explore my new abode.

The island is low and flat, and at high water its surface is only eight or ten feet above the water-line; but the tide here rises and falls about the same height as at the eastern mouth of the Straits of Magellan,—nearly forty-two feet. Within twenty-five feet of our house was a small storehouse and shed, a hog-sty, and a large stone oven. About the same distance further on, was a house for workmen, framed of timber, and roofed and laid up at the sides with bushes; and the sides were banked and the roof coated with earth, an old sail forming the topmost and outermost feature of the edifice,— except that on one extremity of the roof a headless barrel communicated with the fireplace, and did duty very respectably as chimney and ventilator. There were no windows; the men, and whatever portion of light and air sufficed them, found ingress and egress through a door in one end. It was most evidently made for use, not for show; but appeared to be very comfortable, and was neatly fitted-up with berths and benches, a table, and cooking apparatus. Its occupants were eight in number,—three Frenchmen, two Spaniards, an Englishman, a Welshman, and an Irishman; so that, the island having adopted (for a season, at least) a representative of the "universal Yankee nation," may be thought to have brought together samples from a pretty considerable part of mankind.

Besides these human specimens, the settlement boasted of a dog, two mature porkers, and a litter of pigs. Near the house was a large heap of guano, prepared and ready for shipping to England and the United States. The men were at work hard by, digging it up. It lies on the surface of the ground, to a depth of from one to three feet; is dug up and conveyed in barrows to a cleared spot, where it lies in heaps, to be sifted. Stones, feathers, sticks, and other foreign substances are carefully removed, the larger lumps are broken up, and the cleared guano is spread out in a thin layer; when thoroughly dried, it is covered up with planks. The business was carried on by Captain Matthew S. White, an Englishman, who had then been absent for several months at Montevideo, whither he had gone to procure vessels for conveying the guano already prepared, now amounting to some fifteen hundred tons, to market. The time he fixed for his return had expired a month before my advent upon the island, and Mr. Hall was beginning to feel very anxious for him, fearing lest some accident had befallen him, and anxious for himself and his company, also, as they had but a few months' provisions; the island was rarely visited by vessels, and their only means of reaching any port, in case of extremity, were the ship's long-boat, and a whale-boat, both too small to undertake so long a voyage with any hope of safety.

The possibility that my late hospitable friends on the main land might be led, by their high consideration for me, to visit "Holland" in a body, kept us busy during the day, in making preparations to receive them with appropriate honours. Mr. Hall, who was left in charge of the settlement during the absence of the proprietor, observed that Captain White had often expressed apprehensions that the Indians would come upon the island, some time when he was away, and murder all hands. My shipping from them in the manner I had, was not an event likely to dissuade them from the attempt, or weaken their motives for making it. There were two swivels in the camp, which we mounted upon wheelbarrows, to serve as flying artillery. I ground sharp an old whaling-harpoon, and fixed a handle to it; this was slung over my couch; and a large sheath-knife, for use in case we got to close quarters, reposed under my pillow. The Indians were prowling about the shore, probably expecting to see me reappear among them, laden with the rum and tobacco they came after, and which they had earned by boarding and lodging me so long, and by the multiplied kindnesses with which they beguiled the months of my residence among them. It is likely they think, by this time, that I have been gone a long time for it.

Before retiring for the night, we loaded our swivels to the muzzle, and fired them, to let our neighbours know that we had the wherewithal to give them a warm reception, should they see fit to make us a visit. We then reloaded the pieces, each with a dozen or more large bullets, placed them ready primed at the door, and covered the primings, to keep our powder dry. We had six or eight muskets ready loaded, enough to arm the entire garrison, with plenty of ammunition. The dog was tied to the door-handle, to give notice of danger, and the door carefully secured. Just as we were about retiring, Bose gave a portentous bow wow ! but on going out, and taking a survey of the premises, the alarm proved to be false. All was quiet ; and, with a momentary doubt of the sagacity and discretion of our sentinel, we laid down with a sense of security,—first taking the axe into the house, thinking that the cunning rogues might try to burn us out, should they find the efforts to dislodge us otherwise ineffectual. With this final precaution, our faithful sentinel chained to his post, like a Chinese soldier to his gun, we were soon sound asleep. The night passed quietly away, without any further alarm from our look-out, who was of the English pointer breed,—a sleepy dough-faced fellow, better qualified to show the game than to occupy the responsible station to which he was promoted. He was a great coward, but that was not altogether against him ; for, since the law of self-preservation applies to brutes as well as to men, fear would impel him to make some kind of demonstration on the approach of foes, if fidelity did not ; and one kind of demonstration would be as useful to us as another, if only audible.

After breakfast I walked forth, and cast an anxious look through the glass to the northern shore of the main land, to see if the Indians still occupied their position, and whether they were building boats, or making any other preparations for invasion. There they were,— the patient creatures !—still posted in view of our quarters, the English flag flying on the beach. There were several dogs on the shore, and among them I recognised my own ; I almost fancied I could hear him barking. As we brought no dogs with us, I concluded that they had gone back to the main body, and got a reinforcement, with materials for boat-building, and brought my dog for the especial gratification of his affectionate master ; and now he was capering about on the shore, as if to call me back. Having sufficiently gratified my curiosity in this direction, I turned the glass seaward, in hope to view some approaching sail; but the broad expanse was clear,—no vessel to be seen. On the river banks a few stray guanacos were cropping the scanty rank grass, while others, with their young, were lying on the sunny slopes of the sand-hills. The quiet of these animals assured me that their inveterate enemies, the Indians, were not in the vicinity.

Tired, at length, of this sort of sight-seeing, I returned to the house, and, taking our guns, started with Mr. Hall on a stroll up the island, hoping to shoot some sea-fowl; but returned at noon, unsuccessful. The afternoon was spent in wandering aimlessly over the island, killing time. Walking about on the sea-shore, I picked up some clear transparent stones, coated on the outside with a kind of crust; some of them are very hard, and, when broken, cut glass like a diamond. I wrote my name, and place of residence, on a window of our little cottage, with a fragment of one; they are mostly white, some of them of a vermilion, and others of a straw colour; they are, I suppose, a variety of quartz. The shore is in some

places covered with these pebbles to the depth of two
or three feet, on an average of the size of a walnut; the
hardest specimens were not abundant, but I collected
about a hundred of them. I might have picked up
many more, if they had possessed any special value.

A further examination of the opposite shore disclosed
Indians still prowling about, and I proposed to Mr. Hall
to go over, with the men, and give them a sound drubbing. Revenge, I know, is said to dwell in little minds;
if so, my abode in Patagonia must have dwarfed and
contracted my own intellect for the time being, for I
must confess to the consciousness of a desire to visit
upon them some appropriate return for what they had
inflicted upon me. Mr. Hall admitted the ill-desert of
the Indians, and the entire rightfulness of a severe
chastisement; but, not having the same stimulus to heat
his blood that burned within me, he viewed the question
with a more strict regard to prudence, and was altogether
disinclined to undertake so hazardous an expedition; he
dreaded going any nearer to the savages than was necessary. I would, myself, rather have been shot than fall
into their hands a second time; but contended that the
approach of the boat would bring them to the shore, and
enable us to do them a mischief from the boat, without
any necessity of landing among them. True, the Indians
might succeed in getting upon the island some night, and
effect our destruction; there certainly was nothing to
prevent it, if they had the least ingenuity, and a moderate share of courage; but I knew them to be a gang of
arrant cowards, and the reader may judge of their in-
ventiveness by the preceding narrative. The subject
was discussed till late in the evening, and the needful
preparations and precautions were thoroughly talked
over. When about to retire for the night, we went out
and looked for our vigilant sentinel, whose due place, in
right of his office, should have been at the door. Re-
creant to his trust, the rascal had deserted, to take up
his night's lodging with the pigs. He was soon hustled

out of his nest, and compelled to return to the door, there to be tied, as on the preceding night, to the handle. His choice of such mean company greatly lowered the animal in my estimation. While fixing him in his place, we perceived a light on the north shore; it appeared to be carried about from place to place, and was at some distance from the Indians' wigwams. This had much the appearance of preparation for a nocturnal visit from the rascals—a symptom of boat-building. From my observation of their habits while among them, I was convinced that something extraordinary was on foot; they were not much in the habit of moving about after dark, with or without lights, and nothing but the pressure of an unaccustomed purpose could have made them so enterprising now. We uncovered the priming of our swivels, and greased their muzzles, to make them speak in a louder tone of warning and defiance to the enemy; they were discharged with a loud report, that made the island ring, and must have resounded with effect upon the hostile shore. The guns were reloaded, primed, and mounted upon their carriages at the door. The lights that had drawn forth this sonorous demonstration speedily disappeared; the Indians, it was presumed, had taken the hint, and abandoned or postponed their undertaking, whatever it might have been. I well knew their dread of big guns. When I attempted, at first, to persuade them to go with me to Port Famine, the chief reason assigned, besides the superior advantages of "Holland," was, that there were big guns there, which were "no good for Indians." A council of war came to the conclusion that there was nothing to be feared from them that night, and we thereupon retired.

If our careful preparations seem to belie my expressed belief of their cowardice, it should be remembered that they had once fleshed their swords, if not their teeth, in the bodies of some white men, and had held, for a brief period, islanders in their custody; they were numerous, and might so far confide in their numbers and strength as to dare the attempt to wreak their disappointments fully upon our heads. Our caution was reasonable, and, at the time, was not excessive in degree. In the morning we made a careful survey of the premises, exploring all the sheds, and every other place where an enemy could have secreted himself, but made no discoveries. We walked over the island, and examined the opposite shore; but perceived nothing strange or alarming, except that the Indians still remained in their quarters, and that their numbers had greatly increased.

The question of crossing over and driving them off was revived after breakfast, but, after considerable talk, no definite conclusion was reached, and I spent the day wandering over the island, gunning and picking up rare stones, occasionally surveying the coast through the glass. At night no lights appeared opposite; and having made our usual preparations against a nocturnal attack, we decided that if the black rascals did not speedily pick up their traps, and make themselves "scarce," we would go over and hurry their movements. Mr. Hall found his loyalty stirring within him, in aid of revenge. He said it was too much to see that blood-stained British flag flying among such a miserable set of creatures, bringing freshly before his mind the forms of his slaughtered countrymen. This sentiment I was prompt to encore, and to enforce the propriety of an invasion to wrest the trophy from their hands. This was determined upon for the next day, unless they should sooner relieve us of their presence.

The day dawned with a cloudy sky and a thick atmosphere, which made it impossible to see distinctly for any distance. Towards noon it cleared up, and we discovered that our troublesome neighbours were still there. We thereupon set about the necessary preparations for a movement immediately after dinner. Arms and equipments were appointed, knives sharpened, guns put in order and stacked against the house;—the bell rang for dinner, and we ate with appetites sharpened by excite.

ment. But, on going out, and taking a final look
through the glass before embarking, we observed the
Indians catching their horses. They speedily mounted
their beasts, and rode off. Our anticipated valour was
soon cooled. They had slipped away without giving us
a chance to do anything for revenge, for justice, or for
the honour of the captive flag. On the whole we were
not sorry to abandon the expedition, though it seemed
to me that our chances of security were not much
improved by their departure. They would be very
likely to lurk in the vicinity, and to return with full
preparations for crossing and landing upon the island.
Perhaps their movement was only a ruse to put us off
our guard. Such thoughts crowded my mind; but there
was no use in borrowing trouble, and I dismissed
them.

The men returned to their work, and I set myself to
devise some employment. I had become tired of idleness, and offered to assist in the preparation of guano;
but Mr. Hall interposed a decided veto. He wished me,
he said, to make myself entirely contented, and as comfortable as possible. But the sort of life I was leading
was very decidedly uncomfortable; and I entreated so
earnestly to be allowed to make myself useful in some
way, that he set me to make a row-lock for a boat, or a
few thole-pins, or some other trivial things that served
to occupy attention and divert the mind. Then our
cottage wanted a new floor, and some alterations were
found necessary about the premises. When everything
was done and no more was suggested, I was desired to
go a gunning, to vary the supplies for the table, or to
take a basket and pick the tops of the bushes for
pickling. The bushes, which are evergreen, have on
their tops little clusters not unlike barberries, that make
a very fine pickle. Several jars were filled, and
furnished an excellent condiment for our suppers.

Time passed on, and the non-arrival of Captain
White made it drag slowly. I had thought to take

passage in one of the guano vessels to Rio Janeiro, or some other South American port, from which it might be easy to obtain a passage to California. In default of other occupation, the large lighter, which lay up the creek, two-thirds the length of the island, was brought down opposite the house for repair, to be in readiness to load the ships when they should arrive. Their delay threatened us with famine, moreover, and it was beginning to be felt as a very serious matter. To add to our troubles, the scurvy broke out among the men, in consequence of living on salt provisions, without vegetables. They had been recommended, as a preventive, to make and eat freely of the pickle just described; but, either from want of faith in the virtue of the prescription, or because it was too much trouble, they had neglected to do so, and now found themselves in a poor plight.

About the same time, as troubles

"come not single spies,
But in battalions,"

Mr. Hall was informed by the Welshman, who appeared very friendly, that Mr. Morrison, the Scotchman, was trying to prejudice the Frenchmen and Spaniards against him, and inciting the men to mutiny. The man had lived in the house and been treated like a gentleman, and this was all the return he made for the preference shown him. Sawney's goods and chattels were forthwith thrown out of doors, and he was ordered to take his bed and board with the men. He took this descent in the world very much to heart, and when I talked with him on the impropriety of his conduct, appeared quite penitent. I strongly advised Mr. Hall to take him back into the house; for, though he had proved treacherous, it was better, after all, to have him under our immediate watch than with the men, as he might, in a short time, infect the whole company. After much coaxing, consent was given to his return, and he replaced his things in the house with much apparent gratitude.

He was told that he must show himself an honest man, and labour to undo the mischief he had done, if he had any care of his personal safety; for should any trouble break out, and the sacrifice of life become necessary, his would be the first. He faithfully promised, and, I doubt not, exerted himself to allay discontents and prevent any outbreak. With the Spaniards he was successful; but the Frenchmen were more turbulent, and determined on a rupture. They complained that their allowance of food was insufficient, and threatened to break into the store-house and help themselves. Mr. Hall had served out their daily rations of meat, bread, and flour, by weight, according to the directions of Captain White. The quantity I have forgotten, but remember Mr. Hall saying that it was the same as is allowed per man in the British navy. When the bell rang for work the next morning, the Welshman and Irishman alone went. The Spaniards said that they had the scurvy so badly they were unable to work; the Frenchmen marched up to the house, and peremptorily demanded more flour. Mr. Hall met them at the door; and, in reply, told them that they had the same food, in quality and quantity, with all the others, himself included, and that the allowance of the house proved to be more than we needed. None of the other men complained, and their complaints could not be listened to by him. They had all that Captain White allowed, and if they were not satisfied, they could appeal to him when he returned, which would undoubtedly be very soon. Meanwhile he advised them "to be quiet, and do their own business." They left in a very wrathful mood, not to their work, but to their quarters, and to idle away the rest of the day in sauntering up and down the island. They went on in this was for nearly a week, and at last consented to return to duty, under a promise that nothing should be deducted from their wages, which was given as a matter of prudence. It was not thought safe, in present circumstances, to strain authority over them. Nothing occurred to give serious uneasiness, though the men were so touchy and quarrelsome as to raise a slight tempest now and then. On one occasion Mr. Hall had been with three men up the creek, seven or eight miles, after fresh water, which could only be obtained at that distance and boated down to the settlement. While we were unlading' the boat, a row was kicked up between one of the Frenchmen and the Welshman. Taffy, who was a thorough seaman, when adjusting the ropes to the casks, was assailed by one of the Frenchmen with some derogatory remark, touching his seamanship, prompted by his mode of "putting on the parbuckle." The critic attempted to take the rope into his own hands, by way of enforcing and exemplifying his view of the process; and the two were on the point of settling the question in a summary fashion, in a spirit which it required some effort to quell.

The Indians still hovered in the vicinity of the further shore, as the smoke of their fires plainly indicated, and we were obliged to keep up our preparations for defence. There was nothing to prevent them from paying us a visit but their cowardice; and knowing their revengeful tempers, and the tenacity of their purposes—the long-lived malice with which they were capable of pursuing any evil designs—it seemed not unlikely that, smarting under the disappointment I had caused them, their resentment would prove strong enough to overcome their timidity. In this connexion I had an unpleasant thought, now and then, of a hint given them while we were on our way to "Holland." When about a mile distant from the shore, I picked up a bit of plank, and somewhat rashly, in the impetuosity of desire to contrive ways and means to get to the island, in case the islanders could not be attracted towards us, told the Indians that, if we could find two or three more of the same sort, I could bind them together and make a raft, on which I might be paddled over to "Holland." I informed them, moreover, what was the most favourable time for cross-

ing,—namely, at the last of the tide, as the distance to
be passed would be less, and there would be no difficulty in effecting a landing on the island. No additional materials presented themselves, and the scheme
was given up; happily there was no need of it. But,
less happily, it now occurred to me that what I then
spoke in my own behoof might be turned by the
Indians to theirs, to our no small danger, in case a more
earnest and vigorous search should disclose along-shore
more abundant materials for extemporizing transport
craft.

Some of the men became so sorely afflicted with the
scurvy that we decided to land on the south shore and
chase some of the guanaco for fresh provision. Two of
the Frenchmen accompanied us. Just as we were
getting off, their countryman who was left behind came
running to us, with angry jabber and gesture, vocife-
rating that one of them had his gun. He seized it and
was taking it out of the boat, when the party dispossessed of it disputed his progress, and a regular French
fight of kicking and fisticuffs ensued, which we had
difficulty in subduing. At last we got off, but discovered
only a lone guanaco in a hollow between the hills. We
posted ourselves to surround him for a shot. When he
came out I had a fine chance at him as he crossed the
top of the hill, and made quite sure of him. Unluckily,
the flint-lock missed fire, and, before it was possible to
burn any powder, our expected prey escaped. We
cruised about for several miles, and returned home tired
and empty.

The men continued their work as usual the next day,
but a storm was brewing. On the following morning
the Frenchmen marched up to the house, and demanded
their wages. They were told by Mr. Hall that he had
none of the proprietor's money, nor any authority to
settle with them. Then they would work no longer.
Very well, they were told, they might let work alone,
but their wages and rations could not be meddled with

on demand. So they indulged in another season of idleness and mischief. Their first revenge was taken on old "John," the horse. On the second day of their mutiny the poor animal was seen to halt; a hamstring was cut. He was very fat, and was probably marked by them for food, in default of fresh provision. At all events, Mr. Hall ordered him, as he was useless, to be so dealt with. The men's rations were served out, and the rest was laid up in the storehouse for future use. "Horse-beef" has a strong and singular flavour. I had become accustomed to such diet among the Patagonians, though never privileged to partake of so fat a specimen as old John.

Not knowing to what height the mutinous spirit of his men might carry them, Mr. Hall wrote a brief statement of his affairs, and an account of my arrival on the island, and enclosed them, together with what money and valuable papers he had, in a tin box, which he buried at night in a guano-heap. That would certainly be removed on Capt. White's arrival, or by some one else, if he never returned; so that our tale would not be lost, even though we should not survive to tell it. The desperate character of the men,—all but one or two of whom, as we had reason to believe, had left their country for their country's good—and the recklessness of their behaviour, made our situation rather ticklish. Our fear of the Indians, moreover, was not laid entirely to sleep, though all visible tokens of their neighbourhood to us had disappeared. By passing up and crossing the river, they might approach us from the south shore, which was separated from the island by a channel not more than half as broad as that on the opposite side. The bank, to be sure, was steep and muddy, involving the risk that they would be hopelessly bemired in attempting to land; but this was a weak security against them, if they were resolute enough to make the effort. Nothing occurred for several days to break the monotony of life. No work was done; the men re-

ceived their allowances twice a week, spending their
time in wandering over the island. The large boat
needed repairs, but they rendered no aid. We took advantage of high water, rove tackles, and, by the help of
rollers, drew it up high and dry on the land. When it
was finished,—through fear that the men might seize it
and make off to some place northward, thus depriving
us of our only means of escape, if our provisions should
be exhausted before Capt. White's return,—it was
turned over, and the sails and oars were secured, as far
as possible, from depredation.

Old John was devoured, to the partial relief of the
company; but some were still badly affected with scurvy.
Yet we were afraid to go any distance in search of fresh
provisions, on account of the risk of finding Indians
about. The carcass of a guanaco, just killed by the
dogs, was picked up in time to afford a sensible allevia-
tion of suffering, and to replenish our rapidly wasting
stock of provisions. Indians without, discontent and
mutiny within, and the possibility of famine, together,
would have made the island anything but a paradise to
one who had not so lately escaped the purgatorial pains of
a Patagonian captivity. The first of these disagreeables,
however, began to be less vividly felt. We got tired of
sweeping the horizon with our glass in search of the smoke
of their camp-fires, or other appearances suggesting their
vicinity, and gradually relaxed our vigilance. Bose was
released from his sentry duties, and suffered to exchange
such unwilling service for the society of his friends the pigs.
But we still took the axe into the house by night, and
kept our guns loaded. The boat had to be launched
once more, to go up the creek for water. When it was
unladed, we got the aid of a Spaniard and Frenchman in
drawing it on land, to prevent the rascals from stealing
it, by telling them that it needed painting, which was
true enough. The seine was next got out, to see if some
fish could not be had for the improvement of our diet;
but we got what is vulgarly termed " fisherman's luck,"

and spread the ineffectual net on the gravelly beach to dry. Grown desperate, at last, we decided that, Indians or no Indians, we *must* have fresh provisions, if any were to be had, and manned the whale-boat for an expedition to the continent. We landed on the south shore, and succeeded in discovering and bringing down a solitary guanaco. The game was dressed, and we returned to our home in triumph. The two following days were chiefly spent in hunting, unsuccessfully.

In the afternoon of the second day, having nothing else to pass away the hours, I commenced repairing the lighter, but had not been long at work before Mr. Hall came down, with a smile. "Look out to sea!" he exclaimed; "Captain White is coming." I looked as directed, and saw distinctly two sail approaching. A thrill of joy shot through me; I thought no more of work that day. An examination through the glass made them out to be a ship and a fore-and-aft schooner. Could it be any one else than Captain White? The island was not frequented by vessels except for guano; but it seemed very strange to see a schooner, as a vessel of that rig was not adapted to such a service. Mr. Hall began to think it might be some of general Rosas' vessels despatched to drive away people engaged in taking guano on the Patagonian coast. It had been reported, some time before, that he designed doing so. He heard the rumour a few months previous at Montevideo; and also another, that the Chilian government claimed the country, and were determined to hold it.

The little schooner led the way, considerably in advance of the ship. As the vessels approached nearer, they presented a decidedly Yankee look. We watched them with intense interest, as they passed the shoals, and came up with a favourable breeze, under a press of sail. Soon they entered the river's mouth. On passing the north point the schooner stood up, keeping the north shore, and cast anchor. It was evident they were not acquainted with the navigation, as there is a large shoal

ARRIVAL OF THE SHIPS.

running from the upper end of the island nearly to the mouth of the river, and they had sailed within it. On discovering the error, she attempted to keep off, but, in so doing, struck the lower end of the shoal. Mr. Hall manned the boat, and boarded the schooner. She proved to be the Washington, tender to the ship Hudson, Captain Clift, of Mystic, Connecticut,—a whaling vessel, just from the Falkland Islands. Mr. Hall promised to go on board again during the following forenoon, and pilot the vessel into the channel.

I went with him for this purpose; and, as it was calm, the anchor was hove aweigh, and, with the boat ahead, we towed the schooner across the shoal, which at low water is plainly to be seen, but now, at flood tide, had plenty of water. After getting into the right position, the anchor was dropped, and we spent the day on board very pleasantly. The weather held moderate till afternoon. The ship yet lay off the mouth of the harbour, and made slow progress upward. The schooner, the day before, being so far ahead, had only daylight and wind enough to get in; and the ship, finding she would be benighted, as the wind sank with the sun, hauled on and off during the night, and then lay with scarcely wind enough to fill the sails. A smart breeze, however, sprung up in the afternoon, and she came gallantly into port, only repeating the mistake made by the schooner between the channels; but got off at night with the tide, and, after some delay, anchored securely in sufficient depth of water. As she intended making some stay in port, she was subsequently taken further up to the proper anchorage, and was moored on the 5th of October, having come in on the 4th.

Captain Clift had been informed by the mate, who had been ashore, and by Mr. Hall, of my misfortunes and adventures among the Patagonians, and on the following day sent a message inviting me on board his vessel. He received me very cordially, and insisted that I should make his ship my home as long as it should suit my convenience to do so. I accepted his kind offer, first going on shore, and communicating it to my liberal benefactor, Mr. Hall. He at once assented that it would undoubtedly be pleasanter to be with my countrymen. I could not leave him, however, without endeavouring to express my earnest gratitude for my rescue from a captivity worse almost than death, and for the kindly sympathy and generous hospitality that he had exercised for two months. In my destitute condition I had nothing but thanks to give, and I fervently hoped he might never be in a situation to need the like kindness from others; but he was assured, that whenever or however it might be possible to show my gratitude in a more substantial manner, it would be my happiness to do so. He begged me to give myself no trouble on that score, insisted on my retaining the articles of clothing with which he had supplied me, hoped I would come often and see him while the vessels continued there, and I bade this noble specimen of the true-hearted Englishman a tearful good-by.

CAPT. GARDINER'S MISSION TO PATAGONIA

IN 1850-1.

THE immense district of Patagonia and the island of Tierra del Fuego, extending through the last fifteen degrees of south latitude occupied by South America, has always been an unknown land to Europeans. It was first visited by Magellan, in 1519, when he skirted the American coast to discover a passage into the Atlantic; but he, of course bent on the *one* grand discovery that has immortalized his name, could not linger among a set of savages on a barbarous coast. When Le Maire's expedition was fitted out to discover *another* passage into the Atlantic, a landing was effected, and a young tall Patagonian, whom the sailors called " The Giant," was coaxed on board one of the ships, which set sail with him. After they had been a short time at sea, the crew, tired of their long and hitherto unsuccessful voyage, and thinking they could make a handsome sum by the exhibition of "The Giant" in Holland, steered homeward, leaving Le Maire and the rest of the ships to prosecute their voyage. But as the poor giant proceeded northward, the unusual warmth affected him most severely; and before they crossed the line, the unfortunate exile defeated the hopes of the would-be showmen.

The information that was picked up occasionally after this, regarding the natives of the country, resulted in the belief that the Patagonians were a race of stalwart giants, in the lowest depths of barbarism, inhospitable in their manners, and inhabiting a desert, dreary, inhospitable country. No vessels ever sent boats on shore, except for water or wood; and then they were always carefully armed against the treacherous—for they seldom made direct—attacks of the natives. No attempts to spread a knowledge of Christianity among these savages had ever been made; even the Spanish missionaries seem to have been deterred from such an undertaking, though the Spanish settlements bordered the country on the north.

A few years ago, however, a Patagonian Mission Society was formed at Bristol, which sent out a party from Liverpool, in September, 1850, with the highly laudable purpose of diffusing among "those roving clans and fierce barbarians, the benefits of knowledge, and the blessings of religion." They were safely landed at their destination, and the vessel which took them out proceeded to California. From that time till the beginning of 1851 they were never heard of: when Captain Moorshed, of H. M. S. Dido, who was sent out to search for them, discovered unmistakable evidence that they had all miserably perished from cold, sickness, and starvation.

The following account is taken from Captain Moorshed's reports:

The Patagonian Mission party consisted of Commander Allen Francis Gardiner, of 1826; Messrs. Maidment and Williams, catechists; Irwin, Carpenter, John Badcock, John Bryant, and John Pearce, boatmen. They left Liverpool on or about the 7th of September, 1850, on board the *Ocean Queen*, which vessel was going round Cape Horn, and on to California. On October the 4th, they sent letters home by the *Peter Senn*, from Rio de Janeiro to London; and again they had an opportunity of sending to their friends by a Spanish vessel bound to Rio de Janeiro, the 16th of the same month: by the latter vessel Captain G. wrote to Mr. Lafone, at Monte Video, informing him of the destination of the mission

party, and requesting him to permit the vessel employed
by him between Monte Video and the Falkland Islands
to visit the mission at Banner Cove, with supplies, as
soon as convenient. One of the party, named Badcock,
soon after the embarkation, had an attack of fever, which
was prevalent at the village from which he came,—viz.,
Monsehole, near Penzance, in Cornwall; the other two
boatmen subsequently had attacks, which yielded under
the care of Mr. Williams. Mr. Maidment during the
voyage suffered much from sea-sickness. On December
the 5th, the *Ocean Queen* anchored in Banner Roads,
Picton Island, Tierra del Fuego. Between that date
and the 19th the mission were landed, and their boats
got in some measure fit for service. The *Ocean Queen*
left for her destination on that day, as also did Captain
G. and his party in their two boats—one named the
Pioneer, an open boat; the other the *Speedwell*, a decked
one, with two dingeys (small boats). His purpose was
to examine the north side of the channel, in the hope of
finding a secure anchorage not frequented by the natives,
where he might uninterruptedly complete the fittings of
his boats. On getting away from Banner Roads, the
Speedwell touched the ground; the *Pioneer* rounded a
point of land and shut the *Speedwell* in. The former
proceeded with the two small boats in tow, thinking her
consort was following. While going over the north
shore the wind freshened, and the dingeys broke adrift,
and were never recovered—a very sad loss to them. The
Pioneer found, about 17 miles from Picton, a very beautiful expanse of water entered into by a snug cove; they
were perfectly landlocked. It had the appearance of a
lake, the land about was perfectly wooded, green slopes
with ornamental copses of trees skirted its margin, and
altogether it was to the eye a most lovely spot. They
moored to the shore for the night. On account of its
coming on to rain they had great difficulty in kindling
a fire. (It is perhaps unnecessary to state that the
warmth of a fire is seldom unacceptable in these regions.)

This harbour was named by Captain G., Bloomfield Harbour, in testimony of his respect for his valued friend, Sir Thomas Bloomfield. Not finding any symtoms of the *Speedwell's* approach, he became very anxious about her, and resolved to return in search of her; he therefore left at 5 A.M. In consequence of a long beat, he did not reach Banner Roads till late in the evening, when, to his relief, he caught a glimpse of her at the anchorage from which they had started. On nearing her, they shouted with all their strength; but all was still; not a sound was heard but the plashing of the oars and the murmur of the surf on the outer beach. It was an awful suspense. They still approached, and still hailed, uniting all their voices; but no reply: their worst apprehensions seemed to be confirmed, each in his own mind imagining the natives, emboldened by the weakness of the crew of the *Speedwell*, had availed themselves of the opportunity, and overpowered them. When they reached her, no movement or sound was heard, and they fully expected that they had all been murdered. At length a voice was heard from below, which was at once recognised, and one by one their companions appeared. The most gloomy moments had given place to hearty congratulations. It was then 3 A.M., and as Captain G. thought it absolutely necessary the boats should be put in a seaworthy condition, which could not well be done with all their provisions &c. in them, and there being a number of natives about Banner Cove and its neighbourhood, he purposed to effect it in Bloomfield Harbour, where he had only observed an old wigwam, but no natives. Accordingly, that morning both boats started. Unfortunately, soon after, the *Pioneer* became becalmed, and, requiring a little water, he pulled in again to the anchorage, the *Speedwell* remaining outside in the channel. The loss of the small boats caused him to run close in on the beach to get the water: it was then one o'clock, Sunday morning. At daylight they were awoke by the voices of natives, two of whom were preparing to get on board, and to their great concern they found the boat aground, the tide having receded. At this time nothing was seen of the *Speedwell*. It may as well, perhaps, be stated here, that on overhauling their stores after the *Ocean Queen* had left them, they found that *one* item (which, perhaps, might have been the means of saving some of them, if not all)—viz., gunpowder, had not been landed with the rest of their things, and that one flask and a half was all they had in their possession.

To resume the narrative:—The natives alarmed them much, and they were apprehensive of an attack. There they were, high and dry; their situation tempting indeed, if the people had any intention of molesting them. But they remembered Him who, by the mouth of His apostles, has said, "Who shall harm you, if ye be followers of that which is good?" And they accordingly united together in prayer, committing themselves to the gracious protection of the Almighty. The natives observed them attentively, and their manner became more quiet. Shortly after, the *Speedwell* hove in sight; but, on account of the wind, could not get near enough to render them any assistance. After this more of the natives came around them, and some few fish were purchased with buttons, knives, &c.; still they could not divest themselves of the idea that an attack was meditated. However, as soon as the boat was afloat, they were quietly allowed to move from the spot, and they went to join their companions, who had anchored in Banner Cove. There they remained unmolested till the 4th of January, 1851, when rather a formidable force came into the place in different parties—first three, then two, afterwards three more canoes. As they approached, they divided, three coming alongside the boats, while the other two remained near one of their wigwams. Besides the women who paddled, there were two men in each canoe. Thinking so large an assemblage was for some hostile purpose (sixteen men were

counted in all), orders were given for leaving the Cove.
While they were steadily getting ready, bundles of long
oar spears were noticed in some of the canoes; and
while on shore, the natives belonging to the other two
boats were putting baskets of pebbles from the beach
into them. The cables were instantly cut, the stern
anchor hove up; but, on account of their boats having
been lashed together, it was some little time before they
could clear each other and get their sails to draw; the
wind also was light, and they considered the natives
would take advantage of all these circumstances, and
commence what certainly had all the appearance of a
meditated attack. The *Speedwell* unfortunately again
touched ground, and for a few minutes it was doubtful
whether she could be got off. Most providentially, by
means of oars and poles, she was got into deeper water,
and they proceeded out of the Cove. The natives were
observed to be busily engaged in securing the little raft
that had been used for going backwards and forwards to
the shore as a boat, and which was cut adrift when they
started from their moorings. Their intention was to
have gone over to Bloomfield Harbour; but the state of
the wind would not permit it. Lennox Harbour was
the only safe place to which they could go, and thither
they proceeded; meeting, on the passage of twenty-
seven hours, calms, light and contrary winds, and a hard
north gale, which, after they reached Lennox Harbour,
rendered their situation very critical, as they feared
being driven upon the rocks. It being necessary to
examine the bottoms of the boats, they were beached;
but the *Pioneer* was thrown by a sudden gust of wind
amongst some rocks, fortunately without receiving any
injury. The tide was very high when they were
beached; and they were obliged to remain there until
the 17th before they were again afloat. Only two or
three natives were seen there, and they were friendly.
On the 18th they left Lennox Harbour for Bloomfield
Harbour, but when near the entrance they perceived a

large assemblage of natives. Thinking they would not be able to work well in the boats with so many about them, they altered their plans, and went towards Spaniard Harbour, where they anchored on the 25th. The next day they landed, and discovered a river which emptied itself near where they were lying in the boats, which was named Cook's River, in remembrance of the Christian lady who had been so great a benefactress to the missionary cause. Finding where they lay was in rather an exposed anchorage, they shifted on the 29th to a cove on the west side of the harbour (not far from where they first lay), which they named Earnest Cove, in anticipation of the fruits which they prayed might attend their labours in behalf of the inhabitants of those islands. Here their principal troubles and anxieties commenced, and here they ceased; but I must not anticipate. On the 1st of February it blew a hurricane, a heavy swell set into the bay, occasioning a high surf on the beach, during which the *Pioneer* was driven on a small rock in the bay, and then on to the beach, damaged beyond their remedy, the surf making right over her. After this their attention was first given to save, if possible, their provisions, bedding, stores, &c., which was effected at no little risk. All that was saved was removed to a cavern close by, and which was named Pioneer Cavern. This place became the residence of those who lived on shore during their stay in Earnest Cove. They soon found this cavern very damp, and rheumatic pains came on; the tide also at times rose very high, and came some way inside, rendering their position anything but agreeable. For these reasons they hauled what remained of their boat close up to the bank, and converted her into a sleeping apartment. On account of the highness of the surf, they were not able to communicate with the *Speedwell* for two or three days, when they found her and the party on board her all right.

On the 18th of February a very high tide rose again, and

carried away many things out of the cavern, amongst
which was Captain G.'s purse, containing £8 8s. (his
all), his rings, reference Bible, &c.

On the 23rd Mr. Williams was suffering much from
an attack of rheumatism, brought on by having to wear
damp clothes. In order to give him more space in the
sleeping-boat, Captain G. had a shed erected against the
face of a projecting rock, which was afterwards called
the Hermitage. There he resided. On account of the
dampness of the place a fire was kept up. He arose
one morning and found it very low, when all at once it
burst into a flame, and he was completely burned out of
it. The next morning he went to look at his old dormi-
tory, when, to his surprise, he found that part on which
he usually laid his head was covered with large pieces of
rock. A few hours before he had been regretting the
loss of the place; but on seeing the pieces of the rock,
his regret was soon exchanged for a humbling sense of
the compassion of the Almighty in so warning him from
a spot of such danger. On the 17th of March Mr. Williams saw evident symptoms of scurvy in John Badcock,
which determined Captain G. to return to Picton Island,
if possible, for the provisions that were hid in the woods,
so as to enable him to provide better for the sick. On
the 18th Mr. Williams was able to be moved into the
Speedwell, and the wind being favourable they left (the
whole party) on the 19th, and dropped their anchor at
Banner Cove, on the 23rd. On landing the next day,
they discovered in a wigwam a party of natives, consisting of five men, five women, and three children; as
usual, they were importunate, but, on the whole, peace-
ably inclined. The next day they removed in the
Speedwell to Tent Cove, the better to be able to recover
their provisions—viz., one cask of pork and three of
biscuit. On the 26th, Captain G. was busily employed
burying bottles containing notes describing their circumstances, and where they were to be found should any

vessel arrive in search of them. On prominent portions of rock were also painted the words, " You will find us in Spaniard Harbour." Just as he was finishing the last letter, he was surprised by hearing the voices of the natives, and four canoes were seen approaching the Cove. Preparations had been made for a hasty retreat in consequence of the continued illness of Mr. Williams and John Badcock, as also in case the natives should appear in any force. He soon hurried on board, but found that two of the three casks of biscuit had not been brought off, to recover which he thought it would be unsafe to make the attempt. Some few natives came alongside, but their manner was not liked. During the night a strict watch was kept, and a peculiar noise was heard in the wood, which was interpreted into signals which had been previously arranged by the natives. This became a great source of alarm to them. Fortunately, at four the next morning, the wind, which had before been adverse, changed, and they immediately took advantage of it and got away. The natives were observed to be on the alert, with fires lit in their canoes. Some of them followed; but finding the *Speedwell* was too fast for them, they returned. On the 29th they resumed their former anchorage in Spaniard Harbour. On the 21st of April, after experiencing a heavy gale, the boat was removed to Cook's River and secured to the right bank, having an anchor out in the stream ready for hauling off when found necessary. Mr. Williams and John Badcock continued ill up to this time, principally, it is supposed, from a continuance of vegetable food, poverty of blood resulting therefrom. Every care was taken to economize their provisions, and what, under other circumstances, would have been considered unpalatable, was cooked and eaten. A penguin, a shag-fish thrown up on the beach, portions of dead birds, &c., did not come amiss. On the 12th of May they found, that by using the greatest care they had but three weeks' provisions.

Their allowance was then reduced, the strongest using as little as possible, to enable the sick to have a larger quantity.

On the 28th of June poor Badcock died; for some days previous he had suffered much from difficulty in breathing, and had become extremely weak. Shortly before he expired he begged Mr. Williams, who was lying sick in the boat beside him (in Cook's River) to join him in singing a hymn; he then repeated the 202nd of Wesley's Collection, "Arise, my soul, shake off these guilty fears." He sang it through with a loud voice, and then ceased to breathe. On the 30th, after attending the funeral of Badcock, he returned to the cavern; on reaching it, he found Mr. Maidment in the act of leaving, as the tide was then rising very fast, and some of the things Mr. M. had removed further into the cavern for better security. There being no time to lose, they hurried away from it, and had great difficulty in reaching the beach, on account of the surf. Mr. M. was twice taken off his legs. Rain and sleet were then falling. On reaching their sleeping-boat they considered she was in danger of being swept away, the tide being still rising. They then proceeded to the Hermitage, and there they were afraid of being hemmed in, but did not leave it before kneeling down and thanking their Heavenly Father for the mercies they had experienced. They then went into the wood, but the drippings from the trees were worse than the rain that was falling; so that, unable to find any shelter, they remained till 9.30 P.M., standing up or pacing about in an exposed place. With the exception of a very small piece of biscuit, they had had nothing to eat since the morning. They were wet, cold, and hungry; and could not venture to sit down, as everything was dripping around them. At this time the tide appears to have fallen, and they were enabled to get round to the *Speedwell*, where they slept, Irwin insisting on Captain G.'s sleeping in his bed, while Mr. Maidment slept in another man's. The next day they went back to Earnest Cove. On their way they again experienced the care of their Heavenly Protector: near the beach they found a large rock cod, which had evidently been thrown up by the surf. Their sleeping-boat was all right. The condition of the party on the 8th of July was lamentable indeed. Mr. Williams was fluctuating from extreme exhaustion to comparative ease; the rest were daily becoming weaker; so all thoughts of going to Picton Island for the two casks of biscuit were abandoned. They had been rather more than eight weeks on short allowance; with all these hardships and privations, not one word of complaint appears to have been uttered. They placed their full reliance on the mercies of Him whom they desired to serve, by attaching themselves to the mission, and fully expected a vessel bringing them succour would arrive. At this date the remains of all their stock was as follows:—One pound of salt pork, one pint of peas, nearly one pound of tea (damaged by salt water), six ounces of the fish picked up on the beach, two cakes of chocolate, and two mice. They were carefully collecting mussels, which, with the addition of wild celery, had enabled them so long to preserve even the above small quantity of provisions; they being exhausted, nothing but the latter articles, viz. mussels and celery, would remain to them.

I am not in possession of any particulars from the 8th of July till the 7th of August, wherein he (Capt. G.) states in a prayer that the Lord has seen fit to bring them very low, and supplicates Him, if it is his good pleasure, yet to grant them the supplies they stand so much in need of; but that should it be his will that none of the mission should survive, that He would raise up other labourers who may convey the saving truths of the Gospel to the poor blind heathen around him.

The latest date found is the 6th of September: it is a note addressed to Mr. Williams, wherein he says that

Mr. Maidment had left him on Tuesday the 2nd (the cavern was not more than 300 yards from the boat), and had not again returned to him, and doubts not but that he had gone to his Redeemer; that he (Mr. G.) had not tasted food for five days; but felt neither hunger nor thirst. It is very probable that within a very short time after writing the above the spirit of that devoted man was wafted away to the regions of everlasting bliss. In all trials and adversities it is easy to imagine that the words, "It is the Lord—let Him do what seemeth Him best," were ever before him. It appears that previous to this Mr. Maidment had read the funeral service over the bodies of Bryant and Irwin; and it is evident that at the time of Captain Gardiner writing the note on the 6th of September, the only persons he thought were alive were Mr. Williams and John Pearce. That they died at Cook's River, on or about the same time as Captain Gardiner, there is not much reason to doubt.

Captain Gardiner was 56 years of age on the 28th of June, 1851.

Spaniard Harbour is in lat. 54 deg. 53 sec. S., long. 65 deg. 50 sec. W.

EXTRACTS FROM CAPT. GARDINER'S JOURNAL.

May 12 is a note of the biscuit being short; and, altogether, as they have not supplies for more than three weeks, all but the sick go on short allowance.

May 19.—The preserved meat is out, and Mr. Williams appears to be falling.

May 22.—Set apart for special prayer on behalf of the sick, for supplies of food, and the arrival of the expected vessel.

Frequent mention is made of the tide washing into the cavern, carrying away their stores, and endangering their sleeping-boat, which they endeavour to counteract by building breakwaters of stones, but in the night the surf washes away their work of the day. On one occasion I find Captain Gardiner and Mr. Maidment have to escape from the cavern to save their lives, and taking refuge on a rock washed by the surf, they kneel down in prayer.

June 11.—J. Irwin, another of the party, takes the scurvy, and misfortune seems hovering around them; their fishing-net is swept away, and J. Badcock dies on the 28th of June, and is buried on a bank under the trees at Cook's River: after performing the last offices they retire to their boat for prayers.

July 4.—Having been seven weeks on short allowance, and latterly even this having been curtailed, the party was utterly helpless; everything found in the shape of food is cooked and eaten; a penguin, a shag, a half-devoured fish washed up on the shore, and even the salted fox washed out of the cavern, is thrown up again on the beach, and used for food. Captain Gardiner writes:—"We have now remaining half a duck, about 1 lb. of salt pork, the same quantity of damaged tea, a very little rice (a pint), two cakes of chocolate, four pints of peas, to which I may add six mice. The mention of this last item in our list of provisions may startle some of our friends should it ever reach their ears; but, circumstanced as we are, we partake of them with a relish, and have already eaten several of them; they are very tender, and taste like rabbit."

July 22.—They are reduced to living on mussels, and feel the want of food, and sometimes the craving of hunger is distressing to them. Captain Gardiner writes: —"After living on mussels for a fortnight, I was compelled to give them up, and my food is now mussel broth and the soft part of limpets."

July 28.—Captain Gardiner writes of the party in the other boat:—"They are all extremely weak and helpless. Even their garden seeds, used for broth, are now all out."

August 14.—Captain Gardiner takes to his bed; but a rock weed is discovered, which they boil down to a jelly, and find nourishment from.

August 23.—John Irwin dies.

August 26.—J. Bryant dies, and Mr. Maidment buries them both in one grave. John Pearce, the remaining boatman, is cast down at the loss of his comrades, and wandering in his mind; but Mr. Williams somewhat better.

Sept. 2.—Mr. Maidment has never recruited from that day of bodily and mental exertion. The remaining remarks I transcribe literally, and they must speak for themselves.

Sept. 3.—Wishing, if possible, to spare him (Mr. Maidment) the trouble of attending on me, and for the mutual comfort of all, I purposed, if practicable, to go to the river and take up my quarters in the boat; this was attempted on Sunday last. Feeling that without crutches I could not possibly effect it, Mr. Maidment most kindly cut me a pair (two forked sticks), but it was with no slight exertion and fatigue in his weak state. We set out together, but soon found that I had no strength to proceed, and was obliged to return before reaching the brook over our own beach. Mr. Maidment was so exhausted yesterday that he did not rise from his bed until noon, and I have not seen him since; consequently, I tasted nothing yesterday. I cannot learn the place where I am, and know not whether he is in the body, or enjoying the presence of the gracious God whom he has served so faithfully. I am writing this at ten o'clock in the forenoon. Blessed be my Heavenly Father for the many mercies I enjoy—a comfortable bed, no pain, or even cravings of hunger, though excessively weak—scarcely able to turn in my bed—at least it is very great exertion; but I am by his abounding grace kept in perfect peace, refreshed with a sense of my Saviour's love, and an assurance that all is wisely

and mercifully appointed; and pray that I may receive
the full blessing which it is doubtless destined to bestow.
My care is all cast upon God, and I am only waiting his
time and his good pleasure to dispose of me as He shall
see fit. Whether I live or die, may it be in Him. I
commend my body and my soul to his care and keeping,
and earnestly pray that he will take my dear wife and
children under the shadow of his wings, comfort, guard,
strengthen, and sanctify them wholly, that we may
together in a brighter and eternal world praise and
adore his goodness and grace in redeeming us with his
precious blood, and plucking us as brands from the burning, to bestow upon us the adoption of children and
make us inheritors of his heavenly kingdom. Amen.

Thursday, Sept. 4.—There is now no room to doubt
that my dear fellow-labourer has ceased from his earthly
toils, and joined the company of the redeemed in the
presence of the Lord, whom he has served so faithfully.
Under these circumstances, it was a merciful providence
that he left the boat, as I could not have removed the
body. He had left a little peppermint-water which he
had mixed, and it has been a great comfort to me, but
there was no other to drink. Fearing I might suffer
from thirst, I prayed that the Lord would strengthen
me to procure some. He graciously answered my
petition; and yesterday I was enabled to get out and
scoop up a sufficient supply from some that trickled
down at the stern of the boat, by means of one of my
india-rubber over-shoes. What combined mercies am I
receiving at the hands of my Heavenly Father! Blessed
be his holy name!

Friday, Sept. 5.—Great and marvellous are the loving
kindnesses of my gracious God unto me. He has preserved me hitherto, and for four days, although without
bodily food, without any feeling of hunger or thirst.

My dear Mr. Williams,—The Lord has seen fit to call
home another of our little company. Our dear departed

brother left the boat on Tuesday afternoon, and has not since returned ; doubtless he is in the presence of his Redeemer, whom he served faithfully.   Yet a little while, and though . . . . the Almighty to sing the praises . . . . throne. I neither hunger nor thirst, though . . . . days without food. . . . . Maidment's kindness to me . . . heaven.—Your affectionate brother Christ,

(Signed)   ALLEN F. GARDINER.

Sept. 6, 1851.

THE END.

Savill & Edwards, Printers, Chandos-street, Covent-garden,